Beyond Definition

New Writing from Gay and Lesbian San Francisco

Beyond Definition
New Writing from Gay and Lesbian San Francisco

Introduction by
Susie Bright

Edited by
Marci Blackman
and
Trebor Healey

manic d press
san francisco

© 1994 Manic D Press
ISBN 0-916397-30-0
Cover: Scott Idleman / BLINK
Manic D Press   Box 410804   San Francisco   California   94141   USA

Printed in the United States of America
5 4 3 2 1

Library of Congress Cataloging-in Publication Data
Beyond Definition : new writing from gay and lesbian San Francisco /
  introduction by Susie Bright; edited by Marci Blackman and Trebor Healey.
    p. cm.
  ISBN 0-916397-30-0 : $10.95
  1. Gays' writings, American--California--San Francisco.
2. Lesbians--California--San Francisco--Literary collections.
3. Gay men--California--San Francisco--Literary collections.
4. American literature--California--San Francisco. 5. San Francisco
(Calif.)--Literary collections. 6. American literature--20th century.
I. Blackman, Marci, 1963-   . II. Healey, Trebor, 1962-   .
  PS572.S33B49   1994
  810.8'0920664--dc20
                                                    94-12818
                                                       CIP

CONTENTS

Beyond Definition

INTRODUCTION

When I first started sleeping with girls as a teenager, I developed one simple-minded reading interest: coming-out stories. I remember the first, the fifth, and the tenth book of lesbian coming-out sagas that graced my bedstand, and then, just as memorably, I chucked them all out. You see, I was looking for myself in these stories, wanting to find a girl like me, who certainly loved and lusted after women... but who also had a few other things going on in her life, too. I didn't feel like my complications and background fit with the published version of lesbian lives. Those early '70s anthologies were like the King James version of the Bible, and they made me feel like a heretic.

Many years later, I realized my fear that the label was coming before the truth of the matter was no teenage paranoia. It's only been rather recently that sexual lives and erotic identities of all kinds have been candidly described. The typical coming-out story of the past was a white, all-American, middle class, college-educated and politically rarefied document. They usually prescribed a gay life rather than described a sexual history.

Beyond Definition is an entire volume dedicated to stories of sexual identity that weren't visible or understood before, let alone appreciated. Sometimes they come from places that aren't thought of as queer, but then who was it who said, 'We Are Everywhere'? — They are more right on than ever.

Unfortunately, our world still seems to be stuck with irritating labels instead of social comprehension. The other day I was written up for the umpteenth time, by a New York journal of record as "a San Francisco lesbian sex guru." Boy, if anyone seriously told *me* they were a "lesbian sex guru" I would tell them to get a life.

Identifying oneself often involves a short cut, a sound bite instead of a full experience. Maybe if that's all that time allows, we should begin to preface ourselves with, "This is my ID for the next fifteen minutes."

I'll take my next seat as the proud introducer of this anthology whose time has come, to say the least. *Beyond Definition* will be followed by many imitators — I hope they're just as good!

SUSIE BRIGHT
SAN FRANCISCO

Beyond Definition

INDIO
AL LUJAN

Don't roll your eyes at me
I was just trying to tell you that I thought perhaps,
Maybe, I was possibly starting to fall in love with you
Pinche coward
You don't know me or my people

I was ten the first time I told a man that I thought, perhaps, maybe, I was possibly starting to fall in love with him. Indio was his name. He was in Big Hazard, a gang in my barrio in East Los Angeles. He was my sister's old man, she stole him from a chola named La Payasa. He was a fine white cholo. He had the first blue eyes I'd ever looked into that weren't on television. The only blue eyes in my barrio. Hair like dawn's golden blaze. Slicked back, Tres Flores pomade. Crude tattoos down his veiny forearms. Big Hazard. Done in Juvenile Hall. All those fine cholos did Juvi. His teeth looked like those bright white Chicklets they sell at the border. They sparkled when he smiled, which was hardly ever. They crowned his fuzzy goatee. Red bandanna, white tee, khakis, Converse, always. Muthafuckin fine white cholo.

My sister and I would stay up late talking, listening to 45s and making up dances. I remember I made up this dance to *I'm Your Puppet*. It was a cross between these Balinese dancers I'd seen on a film at school and that cholo posturing that still turns me on. It never really caught on, not with the cholos, not with the Balinese. Not even with those fucking dorks on *American Bandstand*.

My sister practiced on me what she would say to Indio later. And showed me how they'd kissed tongue and all on her life-sized Pink Panther stuffed toy. Bumping and rolling, all motion. I took notes. And like that song said, I beat her to the punch.

He was waiting for her after school by the flood control building off Soto Street by my house. My sister, that skag, she was always in detention at Santa Theresita Catholic school for girls. Girls tripping down that road to cholahood. Hell by tenth grade, she was already teasing her hair, reeking of Aqua Net. She plucked out all her eyebrows and drew them back even higher than La Payasa. And La Payasa was chola-controlla.

So I hung out with him between buildings, listening to oldies on his portable 8-track. He pulls out this wrinkled pinner, lights it.

"Quieres? Compra, just kidding, holmes. Toma."

I took the joint, put it to my mouth and took a puff. I really didn't inhale, I mean I was only ten, I just held it in my mouth. Then it all spilled out. I told him that I thought perhaps, maybe I was possibly starting to fall in love with him, and threw in that I thought he was the toughest and cutest cholo in Big Hazard, even if he was a white boy. Those where my sister's words really. I told you I took notes.

He started laughing. Heh Heh Heh... Heh Heh Heh.

And that hurt. It hurt worse than, woooosh, El Chicote, the electrical cord used to discipline my brother and I when we were acting like maniacos.

So he laughed, for a while, and stopped and asked, "You really think so, holmes?"

"Claro que si," I squeaked back.

He leaned over and put his mouth on mine. I reached up, put my hands on his face and pulled him into me. Like I'd seen my sister and the Pink Panther do. He put his tongue in my mouth, filled it. I had to put my hands on his waist because I felt drunk, drunk. He pulled open his Pendleton, folded it, placed it down. He took my hand and guided it around his torso. I felt his hard stomach, his hard chest. I even felt the hair under his arms, of which I had none. He led my hand down to the front of his khakis. And there with my trembling hand, I felt my first hard dick. Also, of which I had none of.....yet. With his free hand he pulled my head down.

A sudden yank at my hair and I was floored. My sister was over me, scratching my face with her knee in my gut. Nearby, my mother, crying, looking skyward, "Porque Jesus, porque?"

Blood ran down my face and spotted the sidewalk like black cherry stars. Blood, the color of my birthstone. Through my tears I could see my brother running towards Indio with a switchblade in his hand.

This was, of course, before the pop of a pistol was such a familiar sound in the barrio. Shit, I would have been the first widowed, pre-teen, gringo-boyfriend-stealing, queer bastard in East Los Angeles. Maybe not.

Indio took off up Soto Street, my brother right behind him, dodging fat women with fat children. And just vanished.

My family moved to South Gate. My sister ran away from home. My brother kicked my ass just about every day. Puto, pinche maricon, fucking sissy, became my new nicknames. My abuelita, who used to call me 'mijo', my son, now referred to me as 'jotito', little fag. This was my grandmother. But worse than all of that shit, much worse, I never got to see Indio, that fine white cholo, again.

So the next time I try to tell you that I thought, perhaps,
maybe I was possibly starting to fall in love with you,
don't roll your eyes at me, man!
Just look deep into mine.
Then look over your shoulder.

A Kiss
Donna M. Lane

well how good can you kiss when you
want to kiss someone the best that you can kiss
where do you put your hands or not put them
and how do you do that with finesse so that the kiss
is as perfect as it can be when you don't know the person
you are kissing that well but you want to leave a mark on them
not a violent mark not an indelible mark but a mark like
you make on a window that is fogged
and someone beside you sees what you wrote

A First Kiss
Ian Signer

I guess it was about three weeks ago that I experienced my first kiss. It was beautiful and terrifying. Warm, wet, dark, and rough, different than I had always imagined it would be. When I met him, I never expected him to do this, to hold me so close, to taste his breath. It made me feel a little uncomfortable, really, yet how could I help but be swept up by my excitement, his firm hands, his deep blue eyes and soft golden hair. At last I understood how boys and girls who hardly knew each other could become a confused tangle by the end of a party or exchange. They, too, had seen the half-closed eyes of desire, felt the rush of blood, the irresistible need to enjoy the endless, formless moments that melt into a throbbing tide of hormones and soft flesh, meeting in the brush of an eyelash, the stroke of two noses as they meet above two joined lips.

It was unreal, really. Like a dream. Before I'd even touched him, the mere sight of him made my blood rush. We talked, and found out how different we were from each other. But with my leg nestled between his two outstretched calves, our hands joined in a gentle clasp, it was impossible for me to think straight. As he left to get beer after beer, I could only think of how unreal this scenario was. In the midst of a torrent of black leather and fuming cigarettes, we were an island. Two young, clean-cut, white boys holding hands, so similar, yet so very different.

Through the fog of this dream, I heard very little of what he said. He was interested in business, he was hiding his sexuality from his parents, he seemed to lead a fairly uninteresting life, and he seemed extremely attracted to my friend, Kevin. Well, I hoped that at least we could be friends, and after some discussion, he gave me his phone number, I gave him mine, and we shook hands in a very businesslike fashion. Then, the discussion took a turn toward our personal lives. I divulged my entire sexual history to him, flatly exposing my experiences, and my innocence. Well, somewhere in the discussion, I mentioned that I hadn't been kissed. Not immediately, but soon afterward, he leaned towards me and planted a small seed of desire on my virgin lips. He immediately backed up, and with a sarcastic glint in his eye said, "Really, no one has ever done that before?" When I said no, except for my mother and sister, he once again smiled and we both enjoyed a nervous, tittering laugh. As the conversation continued, he drew closer and closer. Our hands joined, his head bent over them, like a man in deep prayer or mourning. I could feel his fine golden hairs as they brushed my chin, sending delightful shivers all over my body. My hands slowly stroked the copper fuzz which, flowing out from his arm, slowly trickling and disappearing in the expanse of his firm, gentle hands. When I mentioned something about attraction, that it had to be mutual, those hands gripped me firmly and pulled me close. It was then that I saw those blue eyes, vast and beautiful, falling under the half-closed lids of desire. His mouth was slightly open in anticipation.

Never in my life have I had anyone look at me like that. A deep, longing, and exciting look that made my body swell with passion. When I leaned closer (I honestly thought he was about to whisper something), our lips met. I could taste the faint, stale beer, see the darkness, feel the humid warmth that was his breath. I sunk into the depths of my own longings, and in one short, eternal moment, it was over. God, it was wet. I wiped my mouth, and blushed, recoiling back into my seat like a spring stretched slowly just to its limit and bouncing into a tangled ball that would go no further. I thanked him and gave him a gentle kiss on the hand, only to evoke peals of laughter from a fellow named Frank who sat cross-legged next to us. It was then I realized how many people had gathered in the small covered patio behind the dance floor. He dashed up to get another drink, and I could only sit, angular and nervous, not exactly sure whether or not he would ever return.

PreDahmer
Trac Vu

The first time I ever chewed gum, it was in Sai Gon after the communists took over. Food was scarce. We were constantly hungry. My brother's friend's aunt abroad sent his family a shipment that contained a pack of Spearmint. Strawberry flavor, or something sweet like that. When my brother got back with the loot, it was late at night, a couple of hours after dinner, which we had stretched to no end: five people had shared an omelette made with two eggs and nineteen tomatoes. When I started chewing on the Spearmint, sugar released on my tongue. I wanted to swallow the gum right then and there, eat it like I would a piece of meat. But I knew that I couldn't, that gum was for chewing, that eventually I'd have to spit it back out, in one piece. That's what it was like sucking a guy for the first time.

Notes From A Cocoon
David Harrison

I am in the Roxie Cinema, having just seen a film, and a man strikes up a conversation with me. I say, "Hi, my name is David." After talking for a while, I mention that I'm going through a gender-change. "I'm a *female*-to-male transsexual," I say.

"Does that mean you're becoming a woman?" He looks confused.

"No, it means I'm becoming a man."

When I was five, I asked my mother if I could have a sex-change. She said she knew about male into female, but not the other way around. I used to go to bed every night and pray that I would wake up a boy, and I would always be surprised when I didn't. But dreams do come true.

I was prepared for the physical transformation—as ready as one can ever be, to have an entirely new body. I more or less knew what to expect from watching friends. But I didn't hear much about the other kinds of changes. The emotional, psychological shifts. This first year of transition is the twilight zone. It is so uncomfortable that most transsexuals either can't remember, or choose to forget what it was like. It's because one is always being perceived as something in-between. And there is no place in our culture for that. And while I do feel my growing pains, I also know the joy of a seedling bursting forth out of the ground in spring, and seeing the sunshine for the first time.

It is a new beginning.

I am becoming a man. A transsexual man. How do I learn the language to get along as one in this culture, and still not know what a man is? This gender-change makes me vividly aware of how I was raised to be a woman. I was brought up to put other people first—to support, encourage, heal, and cheer them on—and stay behind them in the background while they stood in their glory. And I was supposed to take heart in having helped them, giving them strength to do it.

There are things I greatly value about growing up female, like the skills to communicate my feelings, and attention given to relationships. But how do I unlearn being apologetic, deferring to others, and making myself small? How do I get to take space, to feel entitled , to feel I'm important, without making someone less so? How do I get that *confidence* that I have a right to be here, that confidence that I'm a whole person? How do I do that when I've been raised to be man's 'help-mate'?

Most talk shows don't talk about *that* emotional stuff. They talk about the hormones, the flesh, the surgery. They call it the 'sex-change operation' as if you go to sleep and magically wake up another gender. They don't talk about how in this nether world, this in-between place, everything comes sharply into focus. When I am beginning to act more like a male is taught to act in this culture, I am acutely aware that I don't know the rules. So, like any teenager, I'm trying on new behavior—tossing out what I don't like, and wearing what fits.

Something that does fit is my new voice. It's the first time in my life that I've liked it. It used to be way up there, sounding to me like fingernails on a blackboard. Now, it's fun. It really is. I sing, mostly to myself and along with radio. When I was a kid I used to listen to the Beach Boys all the time. My favorite song was *Good Vibrations*, and I'd pretend I was the guy who sang bass. Except, of course, I couldn't get down that low. Now I can. I also change the outgoing message on my answering machine, as I hear my voice get lower—which is about every other day—and I always do it first thing in the morning.

The stubble on my face is turning into a five o'clock shadow. There was a time when the thought of hair on me, or anyone else, grossed me out. Things change. Now, some hair on some men is *very* sexy. And I never thought that I'd get so excited watching hair creep up *my* legs and belly, making its ways up, like ivy, to a little tuft right in the middle of my chest.

I'm horny most of the time, and my clitoris is growing.

You know, before I started my gender change a lot of people said to me, "Why would you want to be a man if you can't have a penis?" I used to think that myself. And then I realized it wasn't that important. Don't get me wrong, it *is* important, but I figured I should look at it in perspective. Everyone I know is in some way dissatisfied with their bodies, and so if I get to have MOST of what I want, that's great— since I'm a lot better off than before. Besides, I do have a penis. It's a very small penis, but the clitoris grows quite a bit. When people ask me that question, I wonder if they think a man has no value unless he has a penis, unless he can penetrate someone else. The only real difference physically between me and a man who was born with a penis is that he has the ability to have sexual intercourse. Well, that's not always the case. Some men can't. But of course they don't broadcast it from the rooftops, so no one ever hears about it. They walk around in life and no one knows. Does that make them any less a man?

Within the first month of being on testosterone, one of the first things I noticed was my neck getting thicker. And my shoulders getting broader. And my muscles able to do more than they could before. I have to work out to build them, but I get bigger and stronger more easily. My lover and I like to wrestle and have tickle-fights. One night, a couple of months into my change as I was starting to look more male, we were wrestling. Suddenly there I was, pinning her down. And I was just stunned that I was able to do this, because I never could before—and while I'm being stunned, she's freaking out because, for the first time, she's seeing me as a guy. And I'm on top of her. Right then and there, she was flooded with memories of when her older brother held her down, and instantly she reverted to singing a song from her childhood. She was afraid of me. And now I found myself with a new understanding of what it's like to be a man and have a woman afraid of you because you are man. That was a turning point. That's when I knew my actions were taking on a different meaning than they had before. It's one thing to be pinned down by a woman, but it's quite another when it's done by a man. I have to be that much more aware now of respecting other people's boundaries.

There are times when I don't want to have to deal with any of this, or anything having to do with my gender-change. I'd rather be left alone. Shut everyone out. Have silence. Because every time I interact with other people, I always have to deal with me. You see, inevitably I start wondering how people are looking at me. Do they see a butch woman? I've never thought of myself as butch. Or do they see me as a guy? Or do they just think I'm some freak? One time I went to see a cabaret performance, where there were a lot of lesbians in the audience. A few smiled and checked me out in a way that made me uncomfortable. I was uncomfortable because they were obviously seeing me as a woman—which I'm not—and chances are, down the road a few months, they might not smile at me at all.

When I'm alone, I take off the armor. Sometimes I imagine myself in a cocoon suspended in a safe, protected, comforting place until I'm ready to emerge. However, the difference between me and a baby butterfly is at least they can go into a cocoon and stay there, and not have to face anyone while they're changing. They go to sleep and wake up a beautiful butterfly. They don't have to put up with everyone around them hanging on to them being a caterpillar. They don't have to explain.

Sometimes I grieve for the person I used to be. It's like breaking up with a lover. You will always love them, but you know being together would never work.

The other day I went downtown to get some pants hemmed where I bought them, in the San Francisco Centre. While waiting for the Muni train at Castro Street station, I squat down, leaning up against the wall. I see this person coming towards me. Longish hair in a bob long enough to be tied back. A little taller and stockier than me. White t-shirt, brown denim shorts rolled up. Wide black belt. White socks and thick black shoes. Nice face.

I am trying to be discreet as I look at 'them' out of the corner of my vision. I can't tell what gender they are and that excites me! 'They' are definitely presenting as male—or butch, at the very least. I tell myself it's not supposed to matter, but I suddenly have this *overwhelming* urge to find out. I just *have* to know.

Now we are standing next to one another on the train. I look at the face and notice faint, sporadic stubble around the sideburn area and chin. Less stubble than me, and the rest is smooth. Hands small. If I had seen just the hands I would have thought 'female'. But the chest is flat. Legs about as hairy as mine. I *really* want to know!

We get off at the same station but walk in different directions. "I'm not going to follow," I tell myself as I watch to see if they come up the escalator after me. They don't. Oh well... "Just let go of it."

I go out of the station, into the shopping center and take the escalator up. As I reach the first floor, I see this person again going into a shoe store. Looking at shoes. Are they girl shoes or boy shoes? What kind of shoe store is it? No, I'm not going to follow. I'm going up to the next level to get my pants hemmed. When I'm done with that I browse in a bookstore, buy some shampoo—and check out the shoe store on the way down. One wall is girl shoes. The other is boy shoes. On my way up, I saw the person looking along the boy shoe wall. Okay, well that doesn't leave me with that much more information.

I go out and down the street to get some money out of the bank machine, and then make my way back to the Muni station. As I descend the stairs, who do I see standing on the platform, shopping bag in hand?

I desperately want to say something. Make some kind of contact. But what *do* I say? "Uh, excuse me but are you a female-to-male transsexual, by any chance?" I don't think so.

We get on the same train. We're standing there a few feet apart, and finally I say, "We were on the same train going downtown...did you get something...nice?"

"Yeah, I got a sweatshirt," they say in a vocal pitch not unlike my own.

"Hi, my name's David." I extend my hand. He takes it. "Hi, I'm Brad." His face breaks into a big grin.

After that I'm too shy to say anything else, and I stand there trying to look casual until it's my stop. I catch his attention, and make sure to tell him, "Have a nice day." He smiles and says, "Take it easy," and I get off the train.

It took being on hormones for seven months before I started to pass as a male. Walking down the street now is more comfortable. I relax. I get into the walk, the attitude, the role. I'm creating a persona. I'm constructing an identity. And this one's of my choosing. One close to my heart. When I don't pass—when people call me "Ma'am," when they say "She," when they say "Her," it's like being woken up from a sound sleep by a car alarm right outside my window. It's like being slapped in the face. You see, when people call me "Sir," it's quite natural. So much, that a lot of times I don't notice it. In fact it's been my lover who's pointed it out, "They called you 'Sir.' They said 'He.' They said 'His.' " And when I do notice, I just smile.

I was in a good mood, one day, three months after I started hormones, on my way to see my endocrinologist for a checkup. I'm wearing my sunglasses, my blue jeans, my t-shirt with the sleeves rolled up and a baseball cap. I figure I'm looking just a little studly today... So I'm walking towards a bus stop, and as I approach, I see this man sitting there. He looks at me and says, "How's the economy treating a pretty young lady such as yourself?" Well, that's not exactly what I wanted to hear. I sit down and using some restraint say, "I'm not a lady. I'm a female-to-male transsexual." He looks lost for a moment, and then says quite sincerely, "Gee... I'm sorry" as he gives me a 'man-to-man' jab in the shoulder.

Here I've been trying so hard to look masculine. Even working on my walk. My lover had recently given me feedback that I was looking more 'boy' except for my walk. Something to do with my hips wiggling... So I'd been watching men and modeling my walk after men whose way of moving I liked. But obviously something gave me away. What was it? Was it my face? I had stubble there but nothing significant... it still looked smooth. Was it my chest? I was wearing a jogbra but the larger size, so it didn't mash down my breasts *as* much. What about my voice? It's a lot lower, but still sounding pretty pubescent... But this guy saw 'pretty lady' before I even opened my mouth! What was he looking at? I guess I should just accept that being three months into it, as much as I desperately wanted to, I just didn't pass. But I did come out to this guy. He didn't find *me* out. I felt empowered that it was *my* choice.

That was three months into my change. Five months into it,

things improved a bit. It was at International Male's warehouse sellout sale, and I went off into the changing rooms to try on some clothes. I approach the men's changing area and the woman at the table looks me over, "The women's changing room is over there."

"Excuse me, I'm a *guy*."

"Oh… I'm sorry." So I walk right on into this common changing area with mirrors and lots of guys everywhere, and I get changed. Of course I don't take off my t-shirt but I do drop my pants. Good thing there's a bulge in my underwear. As I'm trying on a pair of pants the guy next to me says, "It's good that *someone* looks great in these clothes." And I'm thinking "Hmmm, why is he saying that?" When I come out of the dressing room I'm happy and excited that someone thinks I looked good. I tell my lover. She laughs. "Honey, that guy was hitting on you."

I have dreams about being in 'Changing Rooms' and getting undressed or changing clothes. I don't want people to see me naked. I don't want them to see that I still have breasts, because then when I get my clothes back on again they will no longer see me as male.

Rooms have significance for people like me. We have to pay attention to rooms. Rooms are given a gender in our culture. Changing rooms, waiting rooms, restrooms.

Have you noticed there's an unspoken rule, that if you're female and don't wear a dress, you're still expected to go through the door with the dress on it?

I always told myself that I would only use the men's room when I started getting consistent feedback that I was passing as male. I was going through all this angst about how was I going deal with it. For a start, I knew I wasn't going to go near the urinals. I had to use one of the stalls. But then what if I sat down to pee? Would people be listening at the door to hear if my pee trickling down into the toilet sounded different? And what if they see that my feet are pointing the wrong direction? And what if I can't pee at all?! I was assured by my friends that many men use the stalls and that I would be okay. I was just told to practice peeing standing up at home, with a modified lid from a tub of Cool Whip. You fold it into a cone to make a funnel. Set it firmly in place and then pee. It takes practice, believe me. At first I just couldn't do it. I had to turn on the water in the bathtub, and I've read the labels on my shampoo, shower gel, and skin moisturizer at least a dozen times. But it's easier now. So with that newly won confidence, I ventured into the men's room for the first time. It was at the airport. I strolled in nonchalantly and went into one of the stalls, shutting the door behind me. I tried peeing standing up. But, doing it for the first time in a public place, not much was happening with that, so I sat down and did it. To my surprise no one seemed terribly interested in what I was doing. It was disappointing. So I flushed, washed my hands, checked myself out in the mirror, and then walked out. To some people, it would appear that I had just used the men's room. To me, I had crossed the threshold into another world.

No Telling
Tede Matthews

On a sunny day
vexed with a chill wind
in a drought
swimming in drenching storms
appeared this person
wearing sunglasses
to guard against the darkness

I couldn't decipher
if she was a
boy or girl

How do you take that
as an intriguing morsel?
A sign of confusion?
Evasion of plot development?
A spy fiction?
A clue to pursue?
A challenge?

Or do you take it like a man?
How does a man take it?
Does he winch
or keep a straight face
when the pain of vagueness
threatens to tear
reason from perception

Or do you take it
prone   on your back

with your legs spread
and your arms flung wide open?
Is that how a man should
take it? And what
is the inherent danger?
Is it safe?
Was it ever?

Why couldn't I tell?
The question remains
of who should I tell
if I could tell
and what is my responsibility
to him   or her
that is   either the listener
or the perceived   if indeed
they are different people
that is   distinct
possessing commonality
yet unique
as in   which sex?
Why only two?

So maybe I couldn't tell
because
the signals were mixed
wires crossed
the ass was a little flat
or the hips in limbo
the shoulders hunched
and the chest hanging
between pectorals and breasts

The jeans
their button fly
capable of imitating a bulge

where a mound might lie
smouldering
An Adam's apple   or
a lump in the throat
Is that a gun you're carrying or
am I just paranoid?

There's always the possibility of snap on tools
left on in a rush
to beat the time clock

Hair cuts relinquished
their social responsibility
years ago
as gender signs
pierced ears   or whatever
went out the same window

And why did I say
she and not he
in reference to
a question mark?
'It' is too rude
too 'other'

I'm prone to use a
universal feminine
as a device
to defuse the overabundance
of testosterone
in daily dis'course

Why boy   or girl?
Not man   or woman?

Have I arrested
that unknown being
in a prepubescent cage
owing to my own uncertainty
or a desire to return
to a predifferential utopic womb?

Have I as witness
claimed censure over my muse?
In the clit/dick dichotomy
where is my refuge?

Possibly I couldn't tell
as in "I won't tell
your secret is safe with me"

As when   in a distant past
my stilettos' echo
once drowned out the uncertainty
of my large hands tipped
with red flames
when projected desire
ignored the obvious
for the need to have

Or is my beard
not a manifesto of masculine perogative
but a sign of maturity
as the woman in me
faces menopause
with a butch stance

COMING OUT DREAM SERIES
Indigo Chih-Lien Som

I.

I dreamt that my mother came out to me. In this dream Asian women dance in a courtyard or in some outdoor public plaza. We step in exaggerated shapes of overdramatic dreamtango. It's a bright San Francisco day with cold wind finding its way through the sunshine. My mother sits at a small cafe table on the edge of the plaza & introduces me to her lover, a younger fortyish Asian woman wearing hip dark shades.

II.

In another dream my girlfriend & I sit on a couch in my parents' house. She is outing me to them. I become enraged. She smirks when she says that I'm bisexual. I tell her to get the fuck outta my house. When she is gone I go back & talk to my Mom who is calm & understanding. Dad is nowhere in sight.

III.

I am alone in Oaxaca with my mother, enjoying the avocados the way only a mother & daughter can. She takes a picture of me in the hotel room with green fingers.

We sit in a restaurant squeezing limes into our drinks. I am overcome with a sudden urge just to tell her everything. Like wanting to jump off a cliff, but knowing you won't do it because that would be so beyond reason, so crazy. But it's the urge, the wish focusing itself in yr stomach, so demanding that you frighten yrself w/ it. I almost open my mouth to say it, but pull myself back from the edge.

IV.
I dreamt I waz hangin out w/ all the girl cousins of mine & everybody was queer. It seemed very normal.

V.
I return from two & a half weeks of travel w/ the fambly. Two & a half wks of confronting unfriendly restaurant menus & young heterosexual couples as common in the streets as gumwrappers. My brother is the only person who hears my daily complaint that Hong Kong does not contain a gift fit for my girlfriend. I am silent over breakfast bowls of jook & on the bus with my mother; I remain mute when my father introduces smiling relatives who want to know how old I am, the unasked question why am I not married yet?

I get off the plane, carry myself home to my girlfriend's perfect arms & sleep. I sleep 15 hours & wake up to a country at war. We are out in the streets for a week together, crying in each other's hair every night from outrage and the sheer shock of war.

By the end of the week it seems farcical to sit in a slick Italian restaurant with my family (including closeted cousin & brother), pretending that half the people at the table are not queer and that none of us ever heard of war.

VI.
This morning my girlfriend said to me, "It's important when you come out to the person you came out of." She's planning a celebration for me, for when I come out to my mom. I picked a date two weeks from now.

VII.

I came out to Mom. I really did. This is not a dream. I am not the same person I was. I am the daughter of a mother who thinks her kids are weird. I dread the in-between waiting time until she comes around.

YO YO
ANGELA GARCIA

I come from a big family, with relatives spread across New Mexico like cattle bones in the desert. Mi familia lives in adobe houses, peeling with generations and bleached by the sun. Sometimes, while walking through the Castro, I look at the rows of quaint Victorians and I imagine myself driving home with my lover. A dirt road leads to the house where I grew up. It looks so silent from far away.

On Christmas morning I lock myself in the bathroom. All of the clothes that I carefully packed for my two week trip back home are scattered on the floor. I've picked through them a dozen times, dressing and undressing, studying myself in the mirror. With each try I see her, Marimacha. That's what I was called growing up. Marimacha: Macho Maria.

"¡Apúrate!" my sister shouts. "Let me in! I gotta get ready too!" I unlock the door and my sister, already dressed and made-up, enters smiling. In her thin teenage arms is her two year old son.

"I told Pedro you were a lesbian," she says sitting on the edge of the bathtub.

"Who's Pedro?" I ask. In the mirror I see her watching me. It is good to be with her again, sharing this small space, two sisters.

"My new boyfriend. He freaked out, couldn't believe it. No way, he kept saying."

"Seria?"

"Yeah. I showed him your picture. He thinks you look like the woman from the movie *Aliens*."

"Must be the hair," I said, reaching for some lipstick.

"I guess. Anyway," she said, taking notice of the clothes on the floor, "Abuelos know you're gay so it really doesn't matter what you wear. Everyone knows."

It's dark in my grandparents' house. I have to squint the sun out in order to see. A quick look around the room proves my sister right when she wrote that my grandmother took down all the photographs of me. Probably she buried them, she wrote. I look to the place where my quinciera portrait hung for years, now just an ugly patch of whiteness on greying walls. How vividly I remember that day, the marking of my official womanhood. I stood so straight in my white cotton dress, conscious of the roses pinned near my breast. After the portrait was taken, Yo Yo came up to me from behind and whispered, "Congradulatios mujer. But too bad," she teased, her lips pouting with lament, "you'll soon have to marry."

Later that evening, when we were alone, with each kiss, over and over, I promised her, no.

The t.v. is on the Spanish channel and mi abuela is sitting in her chair staring at it. Though she hasn't seen me in four years she doesn't get up when I arrive, only takes another sip of her beer. I hug my grandfather and compliment him on his good looks. Smiling, he gestures to abuela. I walk lightly towards her, hoping not to draw attention to my heavy boots. My little cousin notices them anyway and, laughing and pointing, she says, "Como un hombre."

"Hola abuela," I say, bending to kiss her. She does not touch or look at me, but for a moment I wait there, bent towards her, lingering, waiting. I recognize so much of her: her smell of frijoles and beer, her best housedress now stitched at the elbows, the thick gold cross around her neck; her anger.

"Hay chile rellenos y chicharrones en la cocina," she says sharply. "If you're hungry."

My grandfather brings me many chile rellenos. After I've eaten one, he walks slowly to the kitchen and brings me another. This is how we fill our time, all the while smiling, but never speaking.

My cousin asks me if they have chile rellenos in San Francisco. Grateful for the break in silence I answer, "Si, hay comida mexicana, but in San Francisco there are no sopapillas and the food isn't so hot."

"Do you think abuela's chile rellenos are hot?" she asks.

"Ah, si," I answer, fanning my mouth with exaggeration.

"Not me," she says, walking away.

A few hours later, when my sister's son begins to cry, we prepare to leave. While I am putting on my coat I hear my grandmother ask in Spanish if I know about Yolanda Gutierrez.

"What about Yolanda?" I ask quickly, unable to disguise my rush of feeling. For the first time that day, in four years, my grandmother looks at me.

"She is married and pregnant," she says, watching.

Only I could call her Yo Yo. She told me once that was how she often felt, that the movement of our love was fast and spinning, down and up. To find stillness it was necessary for us to hide, to seek out dark places, to shed our Mexican-Catholic skins; in order to touch. But I grew tired of hiding.

When the wheels of the plane no longer touched New Mexico, when I was finally back in flight towards San Francisco, I called out her name softly, "Yo Yo, mi Yolanda."

I could not see the miles of desert below which separated us; it was too dark, too far away. Still, I stared down into the blackness of the small airplane window searching for it, searching for her, for the landscape we made and shared: dirt and flowers, bones and gold. And I remembered her, from child to woman, my first lover, now wife. Her dark hair and eyes. Her name.

BOSTON TO NEW YORK: TREES GONE SWAMP
TIFFANY M. HIGGINS

This is geography of misery. The train clacks into Providence and I think of all I've lost. I used to perch on that hill, struggling alone to not be alone, and so did Ellen. A year after I left she left herself in the river. How many long dead have done just so, in our many centuries of dying in this country.

Wooden pallets stacked. White clapboard churches. Brick old mill buildings, long, bricks over windows, low mist like grits over fields. Swampy marsh water standing, still marinas, water lit pale yellow, spiky reed grasses, poking small, blue cloth sails wrapped tight around the bottom of the cross masts. Hills of shale sloping to the tracks like bunkers for the war we almost don't know we fight on our own lands. Red and white checker water tower. In the underpass, a sudden burst of color, wild letters: fat tags, purple orange mark graffiti. Piles of sand orange cranes paused above. Cars left pale green, undone in the old field, as day lightens. Those simple wooden cross poles for the telephones.

Slocum Garage. Department of Public Works. Stone walls worn away into teeth shaped years ago by curving hands. Close moss on the track bank. Small shoot ground cover flat between beige stones. Gronsberg Bros. Tight scrub in red bog. Boats stacked in backyards. Auto Works, Martin & Son. Marigolds reaching below wires.

THE END OF THE WORLD

IS HEAR

Lily leaves browning almost covering the pond face. A coal car stopped almost unmoving as the flag on this still day. Ferns, yellowing and brown at the bottom, from the rock.

ELVIS WAS A DRUG HEAD
ELVIS WAS A DRUGGIE

The train goes by too fast for me to see if this note's pro or con the King.

Passing through Fairfax County, black janitors sweep projects' fenced-in concrete, while next door, also bordering the tracks, all the workers driving trucks and doing construction in yards are white. This is the economy of poverty in skin color.

Boxes of light, reflected from train windows, move down the hedge line. This is sun imposed on sun.

Up high, orange flowers emerge from white leaves: in the wind, dipping creamsicles.

In the marina, tall masts poke bare as the silvering smooth wood in the neighboring field, a stand of trees gone swamp.

Lucky In Love
Mabel Maney

I'll narrate a narrow escape.

I was having that dream again, the one where I'm lying on the couch and my mother is standing in the middle of the room, trying to scream, her arms flailing about like a shipwreck victim signaling for help. Her mouth is wide open but there's no sound.

She imagined the details of her destiny.

Joe is the man my mother married after my father died one night in his car on the way home from a sales trip; his sample case, best suit and a half-empty bottle of scotch on the seat beside him.

She clutched her purse to make sure the maps were safe.

He was selling shoes that summer; the practical, old lady kind that come in two colors—tan and gray. Tan for everyday and gray for dress-up, we supposed. It wasn't his best job, but it wasn't his worst. "Just you wait until my ship comes in," he said each time he started a new job. "Just you wait."

My mother says that biology is destiny.

What are the stars and when do they shine?

Joe moved in six months later. We hadn't even gotten used to remembering my father was gone. Joe and his couch; a shabby old red thing that took up most of the living room and was off-limits to anyone but Joe. Joe and his slippers, placed just so next to his couch. Joe and his medicine bottles, vitamins and pitcher of room-temperature water laid out in a row on a little table next to his couch.

This place is the center of gravity.

"Are you held together with safety pins?"

Children make Joe nervous. Noise, clutter, dust, dirty dishes, unmade beds, unmatched socks, uncut grass, unanswered letters and wet towels left in heaps on the bathroom floor are all going to make Joe have a nervous breakdown one day.

Rumor has it his mother finally died because she figured it was her only way out. Joe didn't drive his mother to her grave, they say, she gladly ran and jumped in.

"Sort of living in the future, aren't you?"

Whatever possessed my mother to marry Joe is still being debated by the neighbors. It's the most interesting thing to happen on our block since the Drew boy down the street went berserk.

One day, like a sleepwalker who suddenly awakens to find herself at the edge of a cliff, my mother will come to her senses.

What did Mom say dreams were?

I've started keeping a list of everything he says and does to us, in case one day he makes good on his promise to really teach us a lesson. I saw a mystery movie late one night where the victim's diary was used to convict the killer. He had done it with a common household object, the kind Joe is always tripping over and threatening to smash in our faces.

I have a dog.
I have a knife.

Sometimes at night when I can't sleep I imagine the courtroom scene. My mother is dressed in her nice black crepe, weeping into the handkerchief I gave her for her birthday. "I loved those kids like they were my own," Joe would say from the witness box. I usually fall asleep sometime after he's strapped into the chair but before they pull the switch. I sleep peacefully to the sound of Joe begging for mercy.

Soup d'J-Yours
Maggy Merrick

Take Me, I'm Soup d'J-Yours read the title of the ad. I was reading it aloud to a group of my friends one Saturday morning at the Patio Cafe on Castro in San Francisco. It went on to say, *I'm phemme, phifty and phun. If you're butch (of any age—within reason) and you want to play, leave a message on my voice mail and convince me that you're the one for me.*

"Oh, p-h-u-c-k, I'll just bet she's a winner, if you like older lesbians who are so desperate that they have to place an ad in the *Gay Times* in order to get a date." There were times when I would have given anything to take back a less than brilliant remark. As I swilled my latte, I started thinking about the woman who wrote the ad. Something about her words made her come alive. But she had to be some kind of nut to advertise in the paper for a paramour du jour. We finished critiquing the W/W personals, stood up and did our Bradshaw-esque dyke thing. (That's when you hug everyone like you really give a big shit about them.) And then I was off.

I needed to do my laundry and clean my apartment. So I hurried to the San Marcos for some pool instead. At noon the place was fairly empty, but I found a woman who would play. I set up the balls and broke them. I scratched. Sighing audibly, I gently placed the cue on the table. "Thanks," I said, "but when I start off that badly, I only get horrible after that." I'm not really a quitter, I'm just a sore loser. So, I decided to go home and vacuum. That didn't require a lot of skill. I live a couple of blocks off Castro, so the walk didn't provide me with an aerobic workout, but I was still winded given the brisk pace I had set. I vowed to quit smoking as I hit the slight incline. I ascended the front steps of my apartment house, slipped the key in the lock and flopped into my flat. A copy of the *Gay Times* escaped from my pit and fell to the floor, rudely awakening Peebles, my cat, who lay at the edge of my futon—annoyed but immobile.

I was dragging. I fix computers for a living—they brake it, I fake it!—and my work had taken me all over the Bay Area during the last week. I was so glad to be home and not out on the road, content to blink at my beast for the evening, when I realized I'd forgotten to call Cammy to tell her if I could make the movie tonight. Quelle dommage. She'd be pissed. Did I really want to see *Lascivious Lesbians?* This can't be a Cannes Film winner. I'd seen an amateur video one time that cut from some Georgia O'Keefe-like flowers to a nude woman on her back in a garden, then back to the flowers, then back to the nude woman plus another woman with her face stuck in the first woman's pussy, then back to the flowers ad nauseam. If this was going to be another lesbian 'art' film, I could always rearrange my sock drawer.

I dialed Cammy's number. It rang four times and then her tape kicked in: "Hello, this is Cammy, blah dee blah blah dee blah..." She had new age music playing in the background, while she prophetically postulated on the portent of politicians involved in environmental planetary platitudes—puh-leeze!!! I like her a lot, but I get so frustrated listening to her dissertation (a new one every few days) that I usually hang up in a cold sweat, reasoning that my insignificant little message about whose name and phone number I saw on the bathroom wall at JR's could certainly wait until I saw her in person. Or I'd completely forget why I called. "Cammy, it's Cal. Give me a call!" It was all I could manage, before I panicked and hung up. Maybe it's all that New Age/Airy-Fairy music that makes my skin crawl—Eery-Fairy, I should say. So I would do my laundry, take a shower and wait for her to return my call. I opened the lid of my hamper and it was all I could do not to reel from the stench. I guess I'd waited just a teensy bit too long to do all of my gym clothes. I stuffed them into my laundry bag and carted it Santa Claus-style over my shoulder down to the basement—the home of our conjugal laundry room.

I pumped eight quarters into a washing machine, then remembered I forgot to bring the soap down. Shit-er-roo! Oh well, some nice person left their almost full bottle of liquid laundry detergent—no added dyes or odors—on a table in the corner. How thoughtful. I put the correct amount into the running washer, added the dirty clothes and headed upstairs to shower. When I got back upstairs, there still wasn't a message on my answering machine. I stripped, turned on the water in the shower, adjusted it to the right temperature and stepped in.

"Singin' in the rain, just singin' in the rain, what a wonderful feelin', I'm... Raindrops keep fallin' on my head, and just like the gal whose feet are too big for her bed, nothin' seems to fit...shit!" I could hear a voice leaving a message on my machine. I leapt out, body surfing across the wet tile just in time to hear, "Bonsoir, mon amieee! This is the Camster signing off."

"Phuck a duck, Cammy, stop playing tease the drip-dry dyke," I muttered to no one but Peebles. I dialed *69 and got her insufferable tape. At the sound of the beep I yelled, "Cammy, pick up now—I know you're there. Caaammmyyy!!!" A voice deep within me whispered, "Perhaps you should consider listening to your tape, Cal." Oh, yeah. I pushed the button, "Peace on the Planet, Cal. I'm calling to let you know that last night was *Lascivious Lesbians.*" Tonight I'm meeting with my sitar group. It's 5:45 now, and I have to run, so here's the address. You can come if you like. We always have an extra sitar or two." She gave me round-about directions to the Yoga Center. "Peace on the Planet."

As I slowly sloshed back to the bathroom, where the shower was spraying no one, I glanced over at the floor by the front door. The *Gay Times* was still there right where it had fallen. Maybe after I got dressed, I could see what kinds of queer goings-on were listed for tonight. My bedroom was warm from the space heater and I was not really in a mood to go out. I put on a pair of flannel boxer shorts and a long-sleeved t-shirt, went out to get the paper and climbed into a cold bed. I grabbed the t.v. remote and pulled the comforter up for warmth. My pussycat leapt up and landed on the centerfold of the paper. Now I had the remote, the Rag and my ratty old cat for company. I sat up and mauled my pillow behind me, so I could ignore everything in relative comfort.

I couldn't help myself. I turned right to the W/W personals and found the ad. I'm weak when it comes to cute femmes, or even cute-sounding (cute-reading?) femmes. Yep. The ad was still there. Well, I certainly wouldn't call. I'd watch MTV instead. Rod Stewart again. Still. His one-piece body suit outlined every little nook and crevice of his anatomy. I suddenly shrugged. Why not call her tape? It would be interesting just to hear her voice. I could always hang up without leaving a message. I dialed, punched in her ad number and listened. "I'm really glad that you called," she started out. "I like great jazz, cozy chats in front of a fire, and a companion who is not afraid to be vulnerable with me." Her voice was smooth and sweet-sounding. She went on to say, "So, if you sound like that special person, please leave your name and phone number and I'll call you as soon as possible." Do I sound like that special person? Does a bear phart in the phorest?

The tape beeped, startling me, and I said, "Hi. My name is Cal. I'm thirty, live in San Francisco and my specialty is creating bad puns to make my friends groan. I love great jazz, especially Herbie Mann's *Man and Superman* and anything by Cal Tjader. Chatting cozily in front of a fire sounds... well, hot. And being vulnerable with you sounds like a lot of fun." Yeah, I could be vulnerable! "Why don't you give me a call and we'll get together for coffee and whatever." I left my phone number and hung up. It was only 7:27 pm, but I was exhausted by my adventure. So, I decided to turn the t.v. and the lights out and go to sleep. An hour later, the phone woke me up. I reached for the receiver, had a hard time finding my ear and slurred, "Hunh?" into it.

There was a slight pause and then, "Hi, my name is Melanie. You answered my ad." That was quick. Older women sure were desperate. I sat up in hopes that the cold air would hit me and clear my fuzzy brain. She tried again, "Are you Cal?"

"Yes, I'm sorry. I was just... finishing up an important... project for work."

"I'm glad I didn't call earlier. I wouldn't have wanted to interrupt your work."

Yeah, I thought, it would have been brutal if you'd interrupted my R.E.M. sleep. "Oh, that would have been all right," I oozed. "I could have used the break." We blathered along for a few more minutes, and then she asked if I would like to meet the following evening at her place. I said that I would, so she gave me directions. Before we hung up, she wondered why I hadn't asked about her looks. She said that everyone else who'd responded to the ad had asked that question first. I told her that it really didn't matter to me (big lie)—she was a lot of fun to talk to, so I was looking forward to meeting her. She said that all of her friends described her as attractive. Phar out. Were the friends telling the truth, or were they just being kind?

Sunday passed quickly. I ran errands, saw a couple of friends and bathed my cat. The last was a bitch to accomplish. Peebles was not amused. She hates baths, hates me when I give her one, and has trust issues for a solid three days following these encounters of a wet kind. We both survived and I decided that I'd wear a long-sleeved shirt that night to cover the stripes Peebles had inscribed on my biceps in the heat of the battle. And by six that evening, I had showered and dressed. I checked myself out thoughtfully in the full length mirror in my bedroom. "Not too shabby!" I said as I admired my reflection. "You are one cool-looking dyke." I left, walked to my car and headed toward the Berkeley Hills. Crossing the Bay Bridge has been a problem for me ever since the big quake. Every time I get on it, I try to visualize a huge tube of epoxy being poured onto it to hold it together no matter what size trembler we get.

I always emit an audible sigh when I get to the other side. I had made it once more. Now, let the games begin. I was in a playful mood, ready to meet this poor lonely older dyke who needed to advertise for a sexual companion. She would take one look at Yours Truly and beg, "Please, Cal (may I call you, Cal?), take me now! Take me here in front of the fireplace. Don't make me wait any longer." Oh, yes! It would all be too easy. I reached for the Binaca in the little cubby between the two bucket seats of my Toyota MR2, opened my mouth and squirted. I was almost there. Lots of trees and large houses. Looking good so far. I love the hills of Berkeley. I love the Bay Area. I love desperate, older women.

Up and around one narrow tree-lined street after another, and I finally found the right one. A jade green Jag XKE—a classic—was parked out in front of her house. I could get used to this. I parked behind her car, turned off my lights and sat quietly for a few minutes breathing deeply and chanting to myself, "She wants me. She wants me," over and over. Well, out of the car and off to do my civic duty. I rang the doorbell once and waited. Nothing happened, so I rang it again. Twice to make sure it was heard. I hadn't heard a sound when the door opened wide. One of the most gorgeous women I have had the pleasure to admire from such a close proximity stood looking up at me. My jaw hung at an alarming angle, in defiance of years of TMJ work. My mouth couldn't form anything that made any sense. "Hay oh nem!" I exclaimed.

"Excuse me?" She looked concerned.

"Cal," I blurted breathlessly.

"Oh. You're Cal? Please come in. I'm Melanie." I tripped over the door jam and lunged into the hallway. She pretended not to notice as my face and ears turned bright scarlet. She led me into her all-white living room. Plush white wall-to-wall carpet. White satin love seats facing one another. Two white overstuffed velvet chairs. White porcelain lamps. Moonstone and milky crystal knickknacks. She turned around to face me when we got to the center of the room. She reached up, placed her hands on my shoulders and gently pushed me back and down into a love seat. "Wine?" she asked.

"Fine," I replied. I couldn't believe that the only answer I could think of rhymed, for chrissake! She wasn't gone long before she returned with two goblets full to the brim with the darkest claret I had ever seen.

She sat next to me on the little sofa and raised her glass to me. "To our future friendship." I blinked. "Did you say something?" She smiled.

I was still breathing heavily, so I had to force myself to calm down, swallow and look her square in the eyes as I raised my glass to her and said, "This is surely kismet." And I proceeded to pour the wine down my front and onto the satin loveseat. My mouth hadn't been where it was supposed to be. How could I explain? I had to escape. "Send me the bill," I squeaked as I stood up and backed toward the front door, knocking over a three foot jade candlestick that was in my path. It crashed to the marble floor in the hall, shattering the antique piece. "Send me the bill," was all I could say, again. She had a stricken look on her face. What could she say? The damage I had done was irreparable. I now knew how people died of embarrassment. It is not only possible, it is by far the cruelest of deaths.

All the way home, I kept telling myself that I would never again feel sorry for older lesbians. I considered stopping on the Bay Bridge to wait for the next earthquake. The world, I rationalized, should take pity on younger, less wise dykes who need care, guidance and Tommie Tippee bibs to catch the wine!

IF YOU LEAVE A WOMAN FLOWERS YOU'LL PROBABLY SCARE HER AWAY

MICHELLE TEA

i dreamt my pubic hair curled long
down my leg i dreamt
she was so close i could see
the cracks in her lips and
people kept walking in i dreamt
of reading poetry in some hick
country town i dreamt we were
together in this bed that was a cloud,
i turned like a sunflower to her lips
and found a middle-aged stranger,
like the sun went out.
dreams
are like that and life
is like that ten second limbo
between waking up and memory
sounding a dog whistle
to the disappointment
that sinks your chest like a wrecked
soufflé.
i just think it sucks
that she did it at a party,
he said, it's really mean
to break your heart at a party.
she could've done it on the phone
or at least in a place where there
was no one else around,

so i wouldn't have to slip
into the bathroom one step ahead
of crying, sit on the toilet
with my eyes swelling red and worry
about all the whiskey i drank
to impress her, how it is climbing slowly
up my throat like kudzu
and my best friend is shoving
little pieces of paper under the door
with her name on it like a bad dream,
he doesn't know i've just been dumped
even though i wasn't dumped really,
you need a relationship to be dumped you
need a foundation to be dumped off from and
all i had was three long kisses that
spit out hope and poetry like
a catholic woman spitting out babies,
blind to birth control and reality
three long kisses that turned on themselves like
cancer cells, making me need her face
above a cup of coffee telling me
the story of her life and
she says these interactions
are interfering
with getting to know me better,
she says,
the irony.
and all these heartless boys
slumped drunk in a half-empty room
saying you should've just kissed her,
you really blew it, you
should've just fucked her and forgot her—
don't they have souls?
how did they get so lucky
to lose their hearts for good when
mine keeps finding its way back

with a nose like a dog
only to get sucked from my throat
again and again
she's a heartbreaker, this poet warned me,
and this poet should know,
she's got a chest full of cracks
from the girls she let skate across
her heart's thin ice,
i should've listened.
and let me tell you how
there is a full color portrait
of this heartbreaker
chalked in front of her house
by an admiring friend.
she lives on my street.
the world is so small in san francisco,
it is closing in on me
like a necktie.
i step on her face
on my way to the store.

SMOTHERED WITH BOTHER
JANELL MOON

My partner and I try to improve our relationship
go to couple's counseling
she feels I need too much from her
I say every time I want something
she takes two steps back

when the counselor asks me if I love myself
I feel sorry to be here
I get athlete's foot
a deep yearning to be stroked
in damp secret places

my body always feels my feelings
gets asthma when I'm smothered with bother
warts when I get angry
bruises when I can't take life's bumps
once I got lockjaw, only my mouth locked open
a wild yearning to scream and cause a scene

I visualize taking a swing at the counselor
my mind's attempt to avoid vaginitis
want my sweetie and I to leave here
give each other kindness, hold back diabetes
settle on the knee of love.

TWO FREAKS
IN A MEAN GOD'S SWEATY FIST
SPARROW 13 LAUGHINGWAND

next morning over grits and aspirin
i remembered   jack oh shit honey
i can't believe i fuckin did that
convulsive recall cut through whiskey obscurity

                            like the knife
my knife in my hand and jack grinnin it off   just us
friday night drunk again except i was pitbull furied
                about a blank spot
      i was holdin up steel to my lover
      i was serious
what do you mean he asked me at the table
so i had to say before god and my coffee
i threatened to cut you last night didn't i man
more sorries and panicky lovetalk started runnin out of me
until the grin came back   he said oh
that's right   i'd forgot all about it   he held that little smile
so   long i wanted to scream motherfucker but i started cryin

instead
he'd been as loaded as me   didn't know what issue
brought together me and him and the knife and somethin mad enough
                    to shank eight years of us
somethin that backed down when he just said
you know sparrow if i felt like it
i could get really pissed off about this   the movie stopped
there for both of us
he was holdin me while i came apart again

me and him know each other clear
to the marrowbones and black mirrors by now
me and him go on anyway
eight years or twenty thousand
sparrow and jack is the road were goin down
without a simple love poem in sight
                              because we ain't simple and
                                    love ain't simple
love has vicious motherfucker midnights curled up waitin in it
like when we were naked makin war words
about how if
ordinary common people are shit and i hate everyone
i must hate him too
right then i did but he was the one
who said i hate you first and got up to leave
i gave him my back like the finger   told him thanks
for tellin me one piece of truth tonight anyway
and i would have said more but he kicked me off the bed
before i could and if love was somethin simple
it would have busted like a wine bottle right there

it took us two days to cry about it together
but that man has hands that make me forget sometimes
          how much i hate my body
that man can keep telling me i'm beautiful after the first thousand
times i told him that was a
goddamn lie
that man is as smart as me and too weird to ever be boring
with his head full of politics and priestcraft and philosophical terrors
he can tell me about because i've got em too
me and him know each other all right
it's our damnation to
it's our damnation to know that hate walks beside love like a
          shadow that has teeth
it's our damnation each to live in the others
valley of flames

because our demons are crazy drunk
on love for each other
the same way we are
two freaks in a mean god's sweaty fist
it's our damnation practiced to perfection
we've done it for years
we've done it for lifetimes and some of 'em ended like this could have
but we keep comin back
we've got stuff that ruins us for anyone else
we need each others weirdness and rage like dope
it ain't simple   it's got thorns
it's got roots that wrap around bones and boulders
            all the way to the heart of the earth
sparrow and jack is the road were goin down
together in this poem
this car with the back seat full of   monsters
                        that we're always driving drunk
the hit of murder keeps us awake for the ride
sparrow and jack is the road that starts and ends
in the worlds we have where the other one is the only man alive
                        and those are worlds
big enough for all the pain we throw around
because we're men and we can't help it
all we can do is wrap our arms around love
even and especially when it smells like shit and looks like
the black sponge soaked in blood at
                        the center of trust's shattered bones
and around each other after the storms die down

NIGHTLIGHT
CHRISTIAN HUYGEN

"You will not believe this," David said. He rose up on one elbow and touched a finger to my lips. The room was dark. He slipped out of bed without turning on the light and then sank down to the floor on hands and knees until he was just a naked shadow that crept toward the front window and then raised itself up just barely high enough to see over the sill.

"What are you waiting for?" he whispered. "Get over here."

I slid down onto the floor and crawled up next to him on my fingers and toes. I felt like a cat burglar magically scaling a wall. When I reached the window I barely breathed; I didn't want the curtains to move even slightly and give me away.

My shoulder brushed against his arm, and my skin tingled. It's like that when I'm getting to know someone: every new square inch of his skin makes my fingertips drunk.

I looked out over the sill. Four stories below us the street was empty; the dark pavement was slick with recent rain. Most of the windows in the apartment building across the street were dark. I couldn't tell what I was supposed to be looking for.

Then I saw him.

A man was standing in a half-shadowed doorway across the street. Instead of a trenchcoat and fedora, he had on a red and white varsity letter jacket and a baseball cap turned backwards. He was leaning against the wall of the doorway and looking up at something to our right. After a moment I realized that he wasn't going anywhere, wasn't waiting for anyone: he was just *watching*, and we were watching him.

I turned to see David's face. He wore a faint frozen half-smile. "Oh god check it out he's *doing* it," David breathed.

I looked. The guy had a hand in his pocket, and he was clearly fishing around in there. We could see a sizable boner pushing horizontally against his jeans to the left.

The guy must have felt completely invisible on the empty sidewalk.

I could smell David next to me in the dark. Shadowy vanilla and musk and sweat: the smell of a new boy. I could smell traces of me on him too, my own saliva, sour and faint. It would be really nice if I had more control over the traces I leave behind me in the world.

David was half hard already. I reached over and stroked his dick with my hand, the way you might pet the head of a dog you really liked. David mmmmmmed softly and moved a little closer to me.

"Sometimes he spends hours," David said.

David knew a lot about this guy. "Well, if you know so much about him," I asked, "what's he looking at?"

"I *think* it's a different window every night. It's hard to tell. But he always has that church expression on his face."

It was true. He had a preoccupied saintly look. His lips might've even been moving. We were too far away to really be sure.

"Go into the kitchen and watch from the window," David said.

"Are you going to do something mean?" I said. I didn't know David well enough to be able to tell. To me, the man in the doorway seemed like a sleepwalker: he was innocent, he was in a trance, he wasn't entirely responsible for what he was doing. He was someone to be protected, someone who shouldn't under any circumstances be woken up.

David's face melted into a smile at my concern. It was one of those moments when you first realize you really like someone. "I won't do anything mean. I promise... love," he said, and then he kissed my cheek.

So of course I crept into the kitchen and knelt on the floor. The window was slightly open. A cool draft slipped over my legs and stomach and made me shiver. The stove and refrigerator stood waiting, white and almost luminous in the near-dark.

David turned on the overhead bedroom light.

"What the—" I whispered, and crawled back to the kitchen doorway to look. David wasn't invisible anymore. The guy could be staring up at him right now. I couldn't see David and the other guy at the same time.

David was standing in the middle of the room with his back to the window in his t-shirt and jockey shorts. He saw me, grinned sheepishly for a second, then looked straight at the wall in front of him. I got the picture: he was onstage; I was just watching from the wings.

His arms hung lazily at his sides. Then he brought them up slowly to his shoulders, wrapping them around himself. He started massaging his shoulders and neck as if he ached. He closed his eyes and let his head roll luxuriously forward, then around, then back.

I was beginning to really enjoy myself.

"Touch yourself like that," I was going to say. "I like to see you feeling how good and solid your body is. I like you feeling the softness of your own skin." But it was clear that David didn't need any prompting from me. I even started to wonder if the scene in his head had anything to do with me at all.

I didn't really mind. Just knowing that the guy in the doorway might be watching, might even be touching himself too, felt like cocaine sprinting up the back wall of my skull.

David looked up, like someone coming out of a reverie, and wandered slowly around the room. His dick was hardening again, defining itself through the fabric of his briefs like a sun burning its way through mist. You could see the lovely ridge at the edge of his cockhead now; you could see the vein that writes a J on the top side of his dick. David didn't look at me. He found a magazine on the floor, bent down and picked it up. He stood looking down at it, facing the window, and then slowly, like he was underwater, he started turning the pages.

His other hand deliberately closed over the meat of his crotch.

I skittered back into the kitchen. The grimy linoleum was cold under my fingers and knees.

I knelt by the window, raised my head, peeked out. The guy was definitely watching David, and he'd moved—he'd faded back into the doorway. This was virtually an admission of guilt, or else an advertisement of his furtive interest. He was watching our window now, but sometimes he glanced back at the other one, the first one that had caught his attention, somewhere off to my right. I felt like we were on cable t.v. Right then, our market share was bigger than the competition's.

I was floating, abstracted, me looking at him watching my new boyfriend pretend to be looking at a dirty magazine just so I could have the pleasure of watching the guy in the street watch him. The guy in the doorway, although he didn't know it, was the only one among us who had the privilege of watching and being watched all at once. David spoke, soft but firm. "Come in here."

"But he'll see me," I hissed.

"Don't you fucking argue with me, asshole," he said as if the words were natural to him. I heard the magazine hit the floor. When David starts doing a scene he gets carried away.

I got up, brushed off my knees, rearranged my half-erection in my underwear to make the prettiest picture I could, and walked out into the blinding brightness of the room.

David's eyes were a little dull, a little sullen, and his lip curled. The window was a dark rectangle behind him.

He turned sideways to the window and folded his arms. "Where is it?" he said, with an edge in his voice.

I laughed uncertainly and blushed, shifted my weight from one foot to the other. This wasn't a lot to go on. I twisted the bottom edge of my t-shirt between my fingers. "Uhh," I said, "I dunno, man. Where's what?"

"Don't get *cute* with me," he said, and on the word *cute* his hand flashed out and stung my cheek. I winced. He didn't have to do it that hard to make it look real, I thought. Then he grabbed the front of my t-shirt and growled into my face. "I'm giving you ten seconds to tell me where it is. You've got debts around here, buddy. Your slate's not clean."

Now at least I had more to work with. I pushed back. David staggered back a couple of steps. "Stupid fuck," I said. "You're obsolete. We don't need your services anymore. There are plenty of other middlemen around. You're out of the loop." This dialogue was pretty stupid, especially coming from two guys in their underwear, but I tried to forget about that. Our audience couldn't hear us anyway.

David curled his hands into fists and called me a motherfucker. I swung at him half-heartedly. That sent him over the edge: he was a coiled spring leaping free and lunging at me. His eyes were burning with something I hadn't ever seen there before, not even when he was fucking me as hard and deep as he could, not even when he came.

He slammed me into walls, I guess, and stuff like that. There was a certain amount of punching. The room spun and roared. And then I was pinned against the wall with his hands tightening around my throat. I could feel my windpipe buckling. Blood whistled in my ears.

"Kiss me, faggot," he said. "Kiss me like you mean it or I'm gonna fucking kill you dead."

It made sense at the time. That might seem hard to believe. In fact I think that's probably the best thing about David: no matter what he does, it seems to have this weight of inevitability. None of it is open to argument; and all of it makes sense, at least at the time.

I don't know where the necktie came from, but a second later he'd wrapped it around my neck and pulled it tight. I couldn't breathe, I couldn't argue. Mostly I just felt surprised. He'd spun me around so that my back was facing him and my arms flailed uselessly, grabbing at the empty air in front of me. The corners of the room grew blurry and filled up with fog. Right there in the middle of being 'murdered', I splooged. Okay, I was touching myself, but still I came so hard and vast and cataclysmic that later I was amazed the building hadn't fallen down around us.

Before I passed out I had just enough time to wonder how David had managed to maneuver us so that I was facing the window, and the street.

"Let's go downstairs and look for cumstains," David said. He was kissing the red marks on my neck.

"You got carried away," I said. New air burned my lungs. My throat ached. It would ache for days.

He made a little scoffing noise. "You were *there*," he said. "You didn't stop me." I'm not sure what he thought I could've done. David's pretty big.

He stood up and peered out the window. "He's gone," David said. Our little room was dark again. It felt so good to just lie on the floor and breathe in and out. I looked up at David towering above me. I liked the view I had from down there, staring up at his legs. I wished David would trace a chalk line around me where I lay.

"Come on," David said, and held out his hand. It was downright gallant, the way he swept me up off the floor and into my coat and out into the hall where all the lightbulbs but one were shattered and dark. We stumbled down the dusty stairs and out into the street.

When we got across the street I couldn't believe my eyes. There on the sidewalk in front of the doorway were two pale streaks like wet white comet tails. You would've missed them unless you knew exactly what to look for. David crouched down and said "Wow!" and then actually put out his finger to touch them, but I grabbed his hand.

I stepped around him and into the doorway where the guy had been standing. The comet tails were pointing right at me. My head tilted back and I was looking up into our own window. That familiar little room seemed alien and unknowable from out here. Who could possibly live there?

The lights were off. Damn, I thought. I couldn't see a thing.

ANGELINA
STEPHANIE ROSENBAUM

From the moment Angelina walked through the door, I knew she was trouble. Maybe it was the gardenia perfume, the dark roots under the bleach, the mink stole draped casually around her throat. Not that I haven't seen trouble before. In my line of work, you might say, it comes with the territory. I'm a private investigator, a P.I., private eye, detective, gumshoe, shamus—there's a few other terms, but I try not to use them. I hear them often enough, and not from people I like. I've never killed anyone in the line of duty, but I have been shot at. Twice. After the first time I had nightmares for a month. After the second time, I bought a gun. Now I'd never been one for firearms. Hated the smell of cap guns, jumped a mile if anyone so much as popped a balloon in the next room. But I'd be damned if I was going to let some two-bit thief with bad teeth and a worse vocabulary keep me up at night, so I called in a few favors and got a .38 police special and enough ammo to wipe out the entire NFL. Cashed in my Art Museum membership and spent the next twelve weeks at the shooting range, every Sunday afternoon for a whole winter.

But that was three years ago and now it goes with me as easily as a lipstick. While I've had a few sticky moments fumbling for change at toll booths, I've never seen another woman blink at the sight of a pistol among the usual jumble of sunglasses and lint-fuzzed mints. And even the smartest criminal doesn't expect a P.I. to be packing a piece in a Chanel purse.

So like I said, I knew Angelina was trouble. After all, what girl still wears Jungle Gardenia perfume these days? Nowadays they've all got names like Realities or Eternity. Before that it was Poison and Opium. It's only just recently that they're starting to be called Escape. But it was more than just the perfume that got the bells ringing in the back of my head. See, my last two jobs had been working undercover at the register of Mom-and-Pop restaurants, looking to see who had their fingers in the till. Not the most glamorous job, but it paid and I'd always liked waitresses. I'd even lived with one once, back in Albuquerque. It was the eyeliner that got me, the way she'd lean over with that coffee pot, calling everyone "Sugar" in that two-pack-a-day voice while her eyes were far away, back on the reservation she'd run off of and wouldn't talk about.

I'd usually get off work at four, and I'd walk home knowing I'd find her in the bathtub, an eight foot lion-pawed beast of a thing that could have been in *Architectural Digest* were it not marooned in the kitchen of a third floor post-war walkup on the wrong side of Albuquerque. Surrounded by lemon popsicle wrappers and a drift of gardenia bath powder, Dot would be soaking in the tub, one foot swinging over the edge while she counted her tips, reaching over to lay the soggy dollar bills one by one on the radiator, piling up the change in little stacks along the broad lip of the tub. Sometimes I'd join her in the water. Those nights always ended in one of us picking nickels and dimes out of the puddles of spilled Jack Daniels and soggy bath powder.

Everything was fine, in a low rent, Priscilla Presley-ish sort of way, until I looked up from the register and saw Dot leaning over her coffeepot at a new woman who'd just come in out of the rain. Her skin was heavily tanned and dripping wet, and the water was pooling around the silvery points of her cowboy boots—not the thin-soled white-fringed kind, but heavy, black and well worn with the look of the streets but the soul of the desert. That tan got going with those boots and that turquoise concha belt and I knew that Dot had just found the urban cowgirl of her dreams. I wasn't going stick around as they rode off into the sunset. That girl's name was Fayver Love, with a Y and a V, and she wasn't doing me any. Sure enough, come 10 p.m. Dot was slung on the back of her Harley and she didn't come back.

I cleared out the next day, packed my suitcase, picked up my check and hopped the first train back to Union City, nursing a bad hangover and a broken heart. I never heard from Dot or Fayver Love again. That is, until Ms. Love turned up that day in my office, all decked out like John Wayne in drag.

"So what can I do for you, Ms....?" I let my question trail off like skywriting. I wasn't giving anything away. This girl was a smooth operator and even a bad case of '50s nostalgia wasn't going to keep her from changing names with every outfit.

"Angelina. Please. Just call me Angelina. I feel I can trust you... Can't I?" She had this trick of dropping her voice at the end of a question, so that even the most innocuous remark became ripe with innuendo and intimate suggestion. In fact, the whole setup had a New Orleans feel to it, like she was about to pull a gilded cupid or a couple of beignets out of her purse at any moment. I wrenched my thoughts away from the king-sized bed (red velvet canopy, fringed lampshades, and palmetto bugs bigger than Buicks) that Dot and I had once spent a long room-service weekend in, and watched her long fingers twist around the handle of her black crocodile bag.

Angelina. It figured. It went with the baby blues and the platinum waves. But this angel wasn't any closer to heaven than the St. Christopher medal around her neck. At least he had a good view.

"You want to trust me, you can call my references. You can start with the Chief of Police down on Ocean Boulevard. After all, he fired me. Cops remember things like that. It's a pleasure that doesn't come their way too often." I pushed the black rotary phone a couple inches towards her bag which was still rocking back and forth between her palms. Looker as she was, I was getting a little tired of the heart-of-gold routine. I'd always liked them kind of mean, to tell the truth, and this girl acting like butter wouldn't melt in her Cherries-in-the-Snow mouth was frankly making me tired.

"So, Miss.... Angelina." I drew the faintest sketch of quotation marks around her name, "Why don't you tell me what you need my services for, and I'll tell you what I think I can do." Jesus, I sounded like a cheap nurse but I wasn't in the mood to roll over and beg for some little piece of home-wrecking trash even if she was built like the best side of the Venus de Milo.

Rather than answer, she popped the clasp on that crocodile bag and drew out a flat silver cigarette case. No monogram, only a fancy little crest that meant she'd probably lifted it from some Boston boutique catering to anglophile New Englanders hooked on *Masterpiece Theater*. Automatically, I reached for the cactus ashtray on the windowsill behind me, then froze in midreach. That ashtray was stolen, of course. When was the last time anyone you know ever bought an ashtray? Point was, I'd nicked it from the restaurant where I'd worked with Dot—one of those southwestern joints that put salsa even on the pork chops. The same diner where the girl now calling herself Angelina had strolled in cool as you please and roped Dot's heart just like a steer. Nobody had called me "Sugar" or brought me coffee in bed since I'd cleared out of Albuquerque, and now with that same desert heartbreaker sitting in my office, I could hear my heart start humming a pretty little tune called revenge. I was going to be doing Fayver a couple of favors she wouldn't forget.

Luckily, the ashtray in question was buried under a pile of mail order catalogs and an empty shoebox from Frederick's of Hollywood, the pink tissue still intact. With one hand I flipped open the catch on the window, as if to give her smoke some breathing room. I pushed an empty coffee cup her way with the nonsmoker's air of humored indulgence. Once lit, she let the cigarette burn down unattended between her third and fourth fingers. A stall for time, as I expected, but it was time to get down to business. "Okay, doll face. Spill."

She wasn't shocked. She took a deep breath, leaned forward and with both hands flat on the desk said, "It's about my husband."

My years playing poker with J.C. and the boys stood me in good stead, and my eyebrows didn't flinch. Butch or femme, this woman was an old school bar dyke and I wasn't often wrong on that count. I bet she made about as convincing a wife as I did, and I'd had years more practice.

"We've been married a year now. He's been traveling on... business so much lately but he came up with the sweet idea of spending our first anniversary here in Union City, where we first met. He was going to fly in from Pittsburgh, and I drove up from Palm Springs. We were going to have the honeymoon suite again and everything. ...Only, he never showed up. Our anniversary was Tuesday, and here it is Friday already, and I haven't heard a word."

I waited to hear the part of how she'd called home, and chewed her nails, thought about calling his old girlfriend, the redhead showgirl from Elko, Nebraska who now lived in Cleveland, then in fear of losing both her husband and her dignity had grabbed the phone book and hurriedly leafed through the yellow pages to D for Detective, somehow getting busy signals at all sixteen listings before mine. April McQueen, always at home.

But she didn't say any of it. She just batted those baby blues at mine and said, "Oh, how silly of me. You don't even know my married name. It's Mrs. Vincent De Spano."

There weren't many names in Union City I didn't know by now, and even so De Spano would've been a hard one to miss. He wasn't mob, exactly, at least the juries at his last five trials had never been convinced. For all his sharkskin suits and snap brim fedoras there was always an air of cement shoes and backroom card games around him. I'd had friends who'd talked about him to the wrong people, and not all of them were still around to talk. But I'd listened to what I could while still on the force, and was convinced that while Vincent De

Spano was definitely a tough guy, he still had a heart that went pitter pat over a particular kind of pretty face.

"He's a big boy, isn't he? A big boy with a mean streak. You don't find too many of those. Especially not with a taste for baby-faced ballplayers and punk prizefighters. Face it, doll, he wasn't in the market for a skirt and you knew it. And I'd bet you haven't spent the last year making breakfast for the man you love, either."

I weighed letting it slip just how I'd come by that information, but I'd gotten lucky with the ashtray bit and figured I'd hold out on my trump a little while longer.

"Why'd you get hitched, anyway? It couldn't have been love, so what was it? Money? I've heard that famous fortune of his is getting spent fast on rough trade and hush money. I wouldn't think there'd be much left to keep you in sables. Or gardenias," I finished, taking a deep breath in the too hot room.

Now I've seen every trick in the book a criminal or a witness can pull. I'm not known for being an easy mark, but I just can't stand to make a lady cry. I slammed the window down and turned on the fan, then pulled the half-full Jack Daniels bottle out of the otherwise empty bottom right-hand drawer. She didn't even start rooting around in her black bag for a handkerchief, like most women do when they're wearing that much mascara. Either femme drag was still new to her or she was seriously upset. I dug a bandanna out of my own back pocket and proffered it along with the Jack.

For a few seconds she ignored both offerings, then grabbed the bottle without a word and took a couple of swigs, not even bothering to ask for a glass. I watched her head tilt back while she swallowed, and felt an itch to get my hands around that white throat. But whether to kiss her or kill her, I didn't know, so I just leaned back to wait for her to finish crying.

"Come on, doll face, office hours are over. Why don't I get you some biscuits and gravy, side of salsa, and you can tell me all about it?"

SURVIVAL
DONNA M. LANE

I'm a sucker for a pretty face so
when the one in the bookstore
told me I was in her dream I thought
I was being given a present

you'll have to wait she said
when I asked her to tell me the dream
but when she did she was in too
much of a hurry to pause long

on her way to an appointment
I walked with her while she told me
I was showing her my breast in the dream
what did it look like I said

like a hole in your chest she said
well it isn't I said it's just a breast
with a smile under the nipple I've
taken pictures of it with eyes drawn on

my god I've seen amputated limbs
people convulsing peeing and shitting
and vomiting at once burn victims
my breast is nothing like that

but she saw the hole she put in my chest
when I told her I had survived breast cancer
not everyone can handle that
even in their wildest dreams

BRUSHES WITH BARBERS
ROBIN WHITE

In 1985 I moved to London for a while. There came a time when
I needed a haircut so I asked the friends I was staying with where I
should go. They were fashionable people and they suggested a place in
Soho called D-MOB. 'D-mob' is a British contraction for demobilize
which is what happened to troops after World War II. As a hair place
it had implications of stepping out of uniform, getting a wild civilian
haircut after a series of regimental ones. My friends assured me it was
the place to go and even though it sounded intimidatingly cool and not
exactly what I was looking for, I had no other good options, so I called
and made an appointment anyway.

When I got there, as I feared, it was *way* cool. It had rebar and
broken concrete sculptures hanging from the ceiling. The chairs were
antique dentists' chairs, complete with those large mobile circular
lamps which used to glare down from behind the dentist's head as he
poked in your mouth with his tools. I didn't much like the iconography
of power implied by those chairs.

Not surprisingly, I didn't get the hairdo I wanted. This was the
kind of place where they know better than you what to do with your
hair. Demobilized in my chair I described something to the hairdresser,
but like the dentists of my youth he simply ignored my pleas and did
what he believed was necessary. He didn't even cut much hair off, he
simply styled it a little, charged me an extortionate amount of money
and sent me on my way.

"Well! I'm not going there again," I thought to myself as I walked
out.

Before very long, it was time to get my hair cut again. Sometimes
I get to a screaming point when my hair drives me crazy and I have to

get it cut now, this minute. My current hairdresser describes that as the stage when you have "more of a hairdon't then a hairdo." Well, I definitely had a 'hairdon't', or even a 'hairdidn't', and because I didn't know where else to go and because I didn't have much money, I walked down the main shopping street near where I worked and went into the first barber's shop I came to.

The barber's shop turned out to be Greek, run by a son and his father. It didn't seem terribly macho and I was actually looking forward to the silence and anonymity that reigns when men are too uncomfortable to speak to each other. There were no other customers waiting so I sat down in the son's chair which was vacant. I asked him to trim my hair, figuring that the cheaper rates at an ordinary barber shop would allow me to get my haircut more often and so it was less necessary to cut a lot off.

I sat back and looked at the decor. Mirrors, glass shelves, and displays of men's hairproducts: *Vitalis, Brylcreem, Old Spice*. The barber was dark-haired, big-boned, and plain-looking in the way that men are when they are unaware of themselves as sexual objects. He chatted a bit and then we fell into silence.

Now barbers' chairs are always armchairs and there invariably comes a point in a haircut when the barber leans over to do a little snipping on the top of your head and brushes his legs up against your arm lying on the arm of the chair. I started to notice that this was happening rather a lot during this haircut. Was it my imagination? No, I didn't think so.

Well, this was an interesting development. I couldn't see exactly where it was going to go since his father was cutting someone's hair in the next chair and my haircut was almost done, or so I thought. I wasn't really sure if I was interested in him anyway, in fact, I didn't think I was. I retracted my arm.

I wondered if somehow I'd given something away. It's not that I believe in hiding being gay, but in certain kinds of situations I just don't bother to advertise and that afternoon in the barber's shop I wasn't exactly on a visibility campaign. But there was something about the way he kept pushing up against the chair and smiling at me in the mirror that made me think that he thought I was enjoying his advances. I pretended to act dumb, while at the same time paying particular attention to my peripheral vision which was where I could most discreetly observe the barber.

After a while the father finished cutting the hair of his customer, the customer paid and left. There were still no other customers waiting. The father and son exchanged words in Greek and the father left the shop, disappearing up the steps to the street, where, out of the semi-basement window I could see the feet of passing pedestrians.

My hair was already shorter than I wanted, and I kept expecting the barber to stop cutting, but he didn't. He was pushing up against the chair more than ever and I noticed that his pants were bulging. He was obviously quite big.

This was becoming too much of a temptation. At a certain point I put my hand back to where it had been on the arm of the chair and watched my hair falling to the floor. I started to get turned on: my ears were throbbing and my heart was pounding. It occurred to me that I could lift my hand to where if he pushed up against it I would have his crotch in my palm. But I still languished in indecision because of the unexpectedness of things and because I was getting concerned about my hair which was disappearing rapidly. The barber was apparently going to go on cutting my hair as long as he was enjoying himself, and his enjoyment seemed to show no signs of letting up.

Now I wish I could say I had been more decisive. If I was in a cheap porno novel, I might at this point say, "I turned and ripped open his fly releasing his massive, blood-engorged, uncut tool which I greedily drew into my drooling, aching throat," etc. etc. Sometimes my life is like a cheap porno novel—but that day I couldn't change genres and so, fearing imminent baldness, I said, "I think that's fine," and he stopped cutting.

He charged me more than the posted price, as if I was somehow getting more out of this than just an ordinary haircut—which I was, but I hadn't asked for it and he certainly was getting more out of it than I was. I didn't have the nerve to say anything and just paid and left, once again without the haircut that I wanted. Indeed, without much hair at all.

THE RESCUE
LUCY JANE BLEDSOE

The National Endowment for the Arts refused to fund my collection of lesbian erotica, forcing me to take a job in the Financial District, where I copied, filed, and made coffee for Meredith, an advertising exec. Meredith liked me. A lot. On the nights when her live-in boyfriend, Douglas, was busy, she coerced me into going out for drinks. I'd thrill her with lies about my sex life and she'd whine about Douglas.

Have a little compassion for me when I admit that I developed a crush on the woman. I was trapped on the tenth floor of an urban vault, a glass and heavy metal building, surrounded by a secretarial pool wearing glasses with crooked legs and rhinestone implants. The corporate bosses, men and women, had such phony faces I felt I could take hold of the corners and rip them off. That I had the creativity to conceive of and then nurture a crush in that environment says a lot about my vision.

Meredith wore gender bender girl suits on her butch body. Picture a woman who looked like a man trying to look like a woman dressed like a man. I took her long, confidential diatribes against her boyfriend as early signs of coming out, and entertained myself by imagining her in levis, a white t-shirt, and a black leather jacket.

One evening around six o'clock, she and I sat drinking martinis at a Civic Center fern bar. My crush was peaking, but I wasn't so far gone that I didn't feel shame. A fern bar with a woman in a suit and sneakers—how low could I sink? Thank you, Jesse Helms. This garden-variety lesbian needed that grant. At least there wasn't any chance of someone I cared about seeing me with her. To make matters worse, Meredith was in an appreciating-her-boyfriend mood. I spaced out while she blathered, "He's so sensitive. Can you believe he cooks dinner every Wednesday night *and* does the dishes? ...He actually cries more than me at movies..."

Sick-o straight girl, I thought. I tried to steer the conversation back to what a jerk Douglas was. I commented on how *hard* she worked and how *much* she deserved in the way of attention, loving. I urged her to be frank with me, to feel safe with the truth.

She turned the corner then, admitting that it would be nice if Douglas cleaned the bathroom sometimes, especially since he worked only part-time. I nodded meaningfully, staring at her with rapt attention. "Go on," I murmured.

But before she could, a big, mean-looking lesbian entered my peripheral vision. If Roberta Achtenberg frightened Jesse Helms, this dyke would give him a heart attack. Standing with her hands on her hips, about six feet tall and three feet wide, she perused the fern bar as if searching for the best place to set up a tent.

Then I noticed she wasn't alone. A couple dozen multiply-pierced, hairy-legged queers flooded the bar. After stomping around like barn animals for a minute or two, they coupled up and started kissing.

Gratitude exploded inside me. My people had come to rescue me. I wanted to shout, "I'm here! I'm right over here!"

I looked at Meredith who had plastered a good liberal smile on her face. "This is wonderful," she muttered through tight jaws. Her legs looked more gripped than crossed.

Since Meredith was so supportive, I decided to include her. I leaned over and kissed her on the mouth. For a brief moment, her lips responded as if they had a will of their own. Then she yanked back. I hoped she hadn't given herself whiplash. She smiled hard to camouflage her terror.

Poor thing. My crush crumbled into pity.

Someone tapped me on the shoulder. It was the original six-foot Amazon. She planted a wet one on my mouth and I threw my arms around her neck so hard she grunted. By the time I opened my eyes again, Meredith was gone.

FIRST DIVE
CHRISTY SHEPARD

You stood at the edge of the dock,
knees locked tight as you took instruction,
a rare reversal in which I was the teacher.
I was confident, standing calmly
next to you in the heat
of country midday.
I placed my hand at the small
of your back
as if by believing you could,
I might power you off the edge and
into that dive.
I envisioned your full, adult frame
launching off the splintered dock,
your clean hands so like your mother's
pointed together over your head,
praying yourself perfectly into the water.
In a moment, you vaulted,
arching out over the green pond water,
your creamy skin caught for an instant
at the height of your dive
against the blue Mendocino sky.
You plunged gracefully,
no belly-flop splashing, just a few small ripples
circling towards me.
Your face emerged, laughing,
triumphant in your first perfect dive.
I didn't know then the difficulty
of such surrender.

WHEN THE EASTERN GODDESS OF LIGHT TOLD PG&E TO FUCK OFF

MARCI BLACKMAN

when the music finally stopped
i listened to a beacon
followed a road that led not to baghdad
or sparky's

no, when the music finally stopped
i scaled untrodden dirt paths
to the peaks of the sky
and waited
alone
to see the solstice

i didn't think about the way we moved on the dance floor
like two birds mating in flight
wings spread
moving in unison
up and down
my body
crouched
over yours
up and down
the tips of our wings touching
then grasping

i didn't think about the way E makes everything alright
and everybody worth loving
and even though we were bumpin' and grindin' with our wings spread
you still managed to kiss her
and in the end there was E and E made everything alright
and everybody worth loving

no, when the music finally stopped
i perched my butt on a plane high above this sleeping city
nestled between its peaks
laying my head on my imaginary lover's breast
watching the golden gate's lights flicker over the harbor
darkness peaking out from beneath her veil
to glimpse the arrival of the goddess

i didn't think about the words
the fucked up words
after you kissed her
that you just weren't sexually attracted to me
even though you fucked me the night before till i screamed
waking my homophobic roommates
flaunting it in their faces

i didn't think about the way you walked down the street in your
motorcycle boots
and your leather
just a little bit of leather you always said
green opaque eyes
staring out
over chisel-smooth cheekbones
my friends calling you the femmiest butch they'd ever seen

or about the way you shut your eyes when you sang
and how it wasn't pretty
but haunting and penetrating
or about the way we talked about shit and things
'cause that's all they seemed
when i was lying safe in your presence

things like abortion
and how you could see both sides
because you felt life did begin at conception

but as a dyke you didn't want anybody telling you what to do with
your body
and how i argued with you
saying if life begins at conception
then why not with every ejaculation?
and since 'conception' originates from the root word
'concept'
then why not with every unprocreating thought of getting off?

no, when the music finally stopped
i turned my eyes high
toward that red orange fiery goddess
listening
as she rose
as she rose
stripping darkness of her cloak
and telling PG&E not to bother anymore
closing my mind
feeling her warm caress on my face
her cinderous fingers on my lips
quieting my tears

i didn't think about the way we talked about love in the beginning
that neither one of us was into it
and that i had lied
because maybe it wasn't love i felt for you
but it was the strongest i'd felt in an eternity
and sue me if i wanted to build on it

and how in the end i was glad i lied
because even though you were a dyke
you started to remind me
of those redneck motherfuckers i grew up with in ohio
beer bellies hangin' over their belts
and back of the neck sunburns
talkin' 'bout family values

wantin' women with
round little handfuls of breasts
tight little asses
and button noses
everything you rebelled against four years ago

and how in the end i was glad i lied
because you kissed her
and if you knew how i felt...
if you knew how i felt...
or maybe it wasn't this deep thang
maybe it was just the fuck
and maybe i was rationalizing my ass off
and maybe i was in love with you
and maybe i wasn't
but it was a shitty thing you did
you could have at least waited till my back was turned

no, when the music finally stopped
i watched the eastern goddess of light
strip darkness of her cloak
and tell PG&E to fuck off
stop robbin' everybody blind
arresting her ascent
for just a second
to caress my face
touching her cinderous fingers to my lips
quieting my tears

OUR LADY OF FRESH PRODUCE

TREBOR HEALEY

At the organic grocery where he works
they call him Ken
they oughtta call him Keen
for how I wail in this unrequited love

He's dark and gangly S-shaped
He's obscene calligraphy
He's as filthy as the bundles
of certified California organic spinach
that laugh at me from the shelves

He's got the earth coming out of his sallow cheekbones
His eyes swing like spades around the room
which is all soil
—and I'm a weed
I wait for him

He moves like
a cobra
in a melon patch
I can feel his venom
from 30 feet

He came from Oregon
where the faerie holyland is
He's got maple arms
and dark oak legs
He's drenched in sexrain

I wilt like broad-leafed edible greens
Is it the rain?
Or the heat?
Or both?
He's a rainbow either way

Harvest me earth-tearing sower
there's vegetable shrapnel at your feet
and questions about you grow into my ground like carrots
I'll be your pesticide-free crop
your market
and your moon

I write my name
on the back of the mountain
for you

EARLY SOLSTICE
(DIVA IN THE DARK)
DAWN OF AQUARIUS

it's all about walking thru shut down train tunnels in our GO-GO
boots in the middle of the night, seeing broken glass glitter like
diamonds in the moonlight upon emergence, how you say DE-GROOVY,
the rush of air, the end in sight like a bad Irwin Allen movie escape, the
credits could have rolled up over our fleeing shadows, the entire
journey from start to finish, the ambience, 60s Batman Supervillain,
James Bond Spy Chick, Camp Warhol Velvet, Outlaw Party Glamour,
all we needed was some POT and a Ghetto Blaster and we'd have been
fine, Run Away With The Poor And Notorious because we can't wait
for a bus or clomp over the S.F. hills after a night at the Underground
Cinema and FAG PARTIES in rundown flats with sleazy hosts frenching
everything in sight smearing my freshly done face because they can't
believe I, the STARLETTE OF THE SPACE-AGE, bothered to show,
not knowing that I was too broke to eat at home.

LONG LOST LOVE
CHRISTINE BEATTY

In three months I have taken to the needle like a long lost lover. At first, Ruby is pleased that she no longer needs to lock herself in the bathroom to fix, that we can now shoot up together. In a twisted way, it's very romantic. Two desperado lovers, social outcasts who find themselves in love with each other and who regularly inject their problems away, every six to eight hours like clockwork.

Predictably, the romance starts to fizzle. The problem is that I love the stuff so much. When I am full of heroin, nothing seems to bother me for very long. Phone freaks can masturbate at me, tricks can be flaky and insensitive, and people can yell that I'm a "man in a dress" or a "punk faggot" or whatever until hell freezes over—and I don't care about any of it. Queen Heroin is very good to her subjects, as long as they pay homage by injecting her regularly. The problem is the 'regularly' part.

When the hooking is being good to us, then it's no problem getting the dope we need. The level of stress between us is low or nonexistent at such times, and it's easy to be junkies in love. Happily ever after and all that. When the money isn't so good, then things get real bitchy between us, and we go from til-death-do-us-part to I-want-to-fucking-kill-you.

During these periods of impoverishment, each little speck of dope becomes a bone of contention. If one of us has done well whoring and the other didn't do so well, the one who made the money will complain how she has to support her shiftless lover's dope habit. If money is real tight, then it gets even nastier.

Money is real tight at the moment. Rock Hudson has just died of

AIDS, and it's all over the news. Everyone is AIDS conscious right now because every headline, every broadcast screams AIDS in their faces. This has a predictable effect on the whoring business, especially for transsexuals. We're practically starving.

Ruby and I have been dope sick with withdrawals more than a few times since Rock bought his ticket to that great hospice in the sky. We are often broke because the phone has all but quit ringing, the bar is almost empty, and the cars don't stop as much. As a result, our prices have gone way down. I know that I can't blame her for our predicament, and I'm sure she knows she can't blame me, but we do it anyway.

And when the money does get good, are we prudent enough to budget it? Hell no, we do just as much as we can and hope tomorrow will take care of itself. This is especially true of me because, unlike Ruby, I haven't been a transsexual for very long. It takes a lot of dope for me to live with my insecurities and the near-daily critiques of how I look on the street. It doesn't matter how pretty I am, and I am pretty. If someone can tell I used to be a man—or still am, as far as they are concerned—then that's what I hear about. And I know of no greater balm than Mexican brown heroin.

BREAKING
JUDITH FAUCONNIER

Stiffly curled up on the couch in the fetal position you bury your head between the couch pillows. You stay there for a while. You jump off and throw yourself against your bedroom walls, you bang your head again and again. You need music, hard music so you throw your tapes and CDs across the room until you find your Sex Pistols/PIL compilation tape. You stick it in your old boom box at maximum volume. You sing along with Johnny Rotten: "THIS IS NOT A LOVE SONG!" You scream the words. Rotten's ugly voice echoes. You're pogo dancing, slamming yourself against the walls. Rush in your body as you start to smash bottles, the phone, the radio alarm clock, your clay sculptures, your bed lamp, your boom box...

You see your shelves full of books. *The Well of Loneliness* is staring at you. You remember how she said the character reminded her of you. You want to destroy it. You jump at your shelves, kick them, they fall over, you kick the wood panels harder and harder until they break, you keep on kicking. Your right foot hurts but you don't care. You want to destroy. Books lie in clumps on the old wood floor. You form a pile pushing the books in the middle of the room forming a small mountain. You jump on top of the mountain, stomp and kick and stomp and kick. You feel the adrenaline, the energy, you can't stop, you don't want to stop.

You see a knocked over beer bottle, beer slowly pouring out, you pick it up, drink the rest of it. You want drugs, heavy drugs. You don't have any. You don't have any money. You want to feel. You want to feel physical pain so you start punching the wall until the skin on your fist breaks open and starts to bleed. The sight of blood excites you. You suck your bloody knuckles, taste your salty blood. It tastes good. The pain in your hand makes you forget about the pain inside. You want more physical pain. More blood. You remember the blades you bought for the cutter in the kitchen drawer. You bought the cutter the day you decided to frame the black and white photograph she'd given you. You stumble through the dark hallway to the kitchen. You find the blades. They shine in the dark. Their sharpness is appealing and frightening. You think of your friend Cara, the self-mutilator. You finally understand her.

You go back to your room with the blades. You shut the door, sit on the floor against the wall. You start to feel numb. You want to cry but you can't. You hold yourself, begin rocking back and forth. You want to disappear. Death in your mind. You pick one of the blades. You feel its coldness as you brush it up against your arm. You cut yourself a little. You don't feel anything. The blade is so sharp it sinks into the skin, like a knife with butter. It doesn't hurt. You cut tiny stripes from your forearm up to your elbow, then you try your left cheek, the blade dives deeper this time. You're hoping to feel more. You feel your cheek. A little blood on your fingers. You imagine yourself dead in a puddle of blood.

You think of how guilty she would feel. The pain she would feel the rest of her life. You think of how cruel it would be. Then you think about your parents, how they would pack up your boxes, go through your journals trying to understand, how they would say, "She was just getting back on track, everything was going so well..." You start wondering about an afterlife. You wonder what animal you'd be. You think of what a coward you are because you tried so many times to go all the way but never succeeded. You think of how lame it would be to kill yourself after being dumped. You don't want people to think you were that weak. You decide to end your life more unpredictably. You feel heavy sitting on the floor. Your butt hurts so you go crash on your bed.

In your sleep you are dreaming you are walking downtown and a Chinese man comes up to you. He wants to play chess with you. You are happy because you like chess. As you are playing he speaks words of wisdom to you. You are annoyed because he is talking about the joys of life and how to lift up your spirits. He is winning. You tell him you don't want to play anymore. He does not respond. You want to smash the chess set. He calmly says, "Finish the game."

You open an eye. The morning sun in your face makes you squint. You look around your room. You've succeeded at destroying everything in it. Blood on the wall. Your head is buzzing. You remember last night. You are disgusted with yourself. You try to get up but your whole body hurts. The cuts on your face feel like bruises. The kitchen phone rings. You quickly pull yourself out of bed. Maybe it's her you're thinking.

I'm a Lot More Stable Than I Used to Be

Ali Liebegott

I.
"what a moving album," they said
as they listened in disbelief
about a woman who was raped so many times
she could hardly spell her name
pressing her nails into the palms of her hands
trying to stay alive,
to clean her house
amidst the memories—
mental and body.

"I mean she wheezed so gracefully," they said
as he shoved her face into the wall,
gripping and twisting her trash bag throat
sealing in the pungent odors
before lugging her to the curb.

"her whole struggle, tragic—yet feminine," they said
as he put her in an official police choke hold
in the lobby of their apartment building
saying,
i see you with your girlfriend
YOU FUCKING DYKE
and it's not like you can't get a man
YOU FUCKING DYKE

II.
and on the police report
where even lynchings and firebombings
don't constitute hate crimes

(you see)
he raped her in self-defense
he told her to go suck some pussy
in order to defend himself
he punched her in the head
and he kicked her in the groin
to try and keep himself alive
(even though he was 150 pounds heavier
and a foot and a half taller)
if he hadn't done it
she might have kicked the shit out of him.
and on the police report
it didn't say why he tried to fuck her
with his hand
as if she'd like it or want it
or need it
OR WHATEVER THE HELL HE THOUGHT
HER LOVING ANOTHER WOMAN
HAD TO DO WITH HIM.

III.
oh here we go again
another woman as the victim
and these damn bulldykes with their combat boots
and strap-on dicks
they want to adopt kids
get married
buy soup.
and here we go again
another victim poem
another victim scene
when i throw my burning victim body
onto your dining room table
rolling around in your turkey pot pie
on this columbus day
on this Knights of Columbus Quincentennial Ball Day.

let's all have a toast and celebrate genocide
how did it go again?
first Columbus begged this woman for a boat
and some money
and told her he'd bring her all this shit
you couldn't find at the indoor swap meet,
but really he was killing people
and fucking sheep for a couple of years
but he told her
he got lost
that's why he was late getting back,
or something like that.
i can't really remember
i was drunk in high school
when were learning it,
or was it junior high
or pre-school
some substantial period of my life
when i found it necessary to get blotto
and cut my body up like pieces of stale cake
and bleed all over my history book
because all i could really manage to do
was cry over dead friends
and read junk newspapers saying:
LESBIAN THIS
LESBIAN THAT
DRAG QUEEN, FAG LADY, COCKSUCKER.
apparently,
they found this lesbian in the snow
that was dated to be over ten million years old
and she was wearing big black combat boots
and had really short hair
and they dug her out of her s/m ice dungeon
which was filled with ancient ice dildos
that she used for molesting kids
because all homos fuck kids

or they dress up like liberace and act like queens.
it's true,
i read it in the tabloid.
it's true,
conspiring minds want to know.
there those radical lesbian bulldyke fag ladies
go again
talking shit and generalizations
about us stock brokers
about us politicians

IV.
"what a moving album," they said
as they listened in disbelief
about a child who was beaten so many times
it could hardly admit it happened
who ducked shovels circling heads
like helicopter blades
who grows up and says
i'm a lot more stable than i used to be
now i only want to kill myself
when i can't decide what to have for dinner

V.
here i am
throwing myself through the office doors
of these poetry journal editors
what we are looking for is poetry about leaves and trees,
that reflects MAN'S STRUGGLE for self-knowledge
and his triumphant lust for women.
we are looking for a 900,000 page anthology
with the cultures and countries we want represented
full of poems about leaves and trees,
with the exception of antarctica where we will substitute
a poem about white glistening snow.
dear poetry editor

i hope you find my poetry acceptable for your
leaf and tree extravaganza—
it goes like this:

i love the way the autumn oak leaf
is red and gold and brown and
CRISPPPP
it reminds me of
the red and gold and brown dog we had
that was always nice
and not only did he never shit or piss in the house
but, he never shit or pissed at all
and when we purposefully fed him food that
was lacking vitamins essential to dogs
how brittle the bones in his tail would get
how crispppppp
and easy they were to snap
when he got dog hair on something.
i love the way the red and gold and brown autumn leaf
crunches
and how when bologna got old in our meat drawer
it would look like an autumn leaf
but not taste as good.
and i love the way leaves rustle when i drag my feet
through them on the way to grandma's house.
the rustling reminds me of the night i remembered
what she did to me
and how i dragged my knuckles
across every brick wall in the mission
the skin rustling
off the bone
the blood
rustling between my fingers
as i rustled majestically toward oncoming traffic...

despite that grandma could be sadistic
and threatened me with a wooden monkey-shaped paddle
that had real teeth on it
and used to scrub me down in the shower
when i was bad
or gave us baths in the sink even though
we were way too big to be in it
she was always nice and warm, like sweaters.
autumn reminds me of how when i walk down the streets
in my city
every day there are more and more homeless people
sleeping on pretty leaves
there they sleep under nice trees
how majestic those trees are
how majestic our big buildings look
how majestic our new florida palms
look in california
the palm trees that cost lots of money
to draw the tourists even further in
leaves and trees that float away
like those big soda advertisements they want to put in space
so we can run from the city to the beach
trying not to follow virginia woolf into the ocean
with rocks in our pockets
so we can
try to calm ourselves
fall backwards into sand
look up and see a fucking soda billboard
floating near the moon!
i see this and walk steadily toward the water
i know i've reached my bullshit quota...
it is time to go under.

VI.

how we stand around while the politicians fuck us slowly
and it is especially uncomfortable for us lesbians
who don't want to be fucked by men anyway
and not only do we have to stand around and get fucked
by our president who supports gays
but goes out of town the weekend they have a giant civil
rights march
but that's o.k. because this is the first president who
cares
at least the politicians are making promises
and breaking them now
they used to not even acknowledge we existed, this woman
said
at least we are getting lied to, i said
that is better than nothing at all.

VII.

i remember the birth of my cynicism like a delicious dessert
melting in my mouth like flan
and how i hated flan at first
how it was an acquired taste
like watching victims running down the street on fire
you can see them bruised and raped and walking like
they've been threatened
been sworn to secrecy.
because this is mainstream america
where the bastards rape the babies
and make them witness murders and fuck some twisted
cult leader
even though they are only eleven or four or not even born
yet
it is a victim world
it is a victim woman

going on about her victim self
well watch me throw my burning victim body
through your white house doors
onto your white house hardwood floors
rolling around
in feathers
on fire
smiling
and screaming
do not ignore my flaming body
molested cunt
scarred arms
lesbianism
do not extend your arm to me offering basic civil rights
and then demand i'm silent
and then demand I AM SILENT.
i am here to burn on your floor
stain your oriental rug
leather couch
gucci suit
i am here to get my waitress hands
all over your walls
and scrub the grease and eggs and grease
and menial labor bullshit angst all over your face
i am here to talk to you about waiting tables
on a party of twelve at three in the morning
and how they do nothing but drool and vomit,
and then re-order wheat toast.
i am here to tell you about
the way city money
is spent on beautification before the people,
and how women are being beaten
and i am telling you
because it doesn't seem that you are aware
of the poverty, and the living standards
because i am sure if you knew

if you saw someone waiting in the shadows
with a baseball bat hammered full of razors
timing the leap into your face

there would be more protection
there would be more funding
there would be more color leaking in those
white house doors,
saying, i'm a lot more stable than i used to be
now i only want to kill myself when i can't decide
how to plan my revolution.

SEX WITH THE DAMNED
(FOR AN ARTIST FRIEND)
MERLE TOFER

In the middle of a skinny room
i reveled in his likeness of Michelangelo's David
a mild shudder of passiveness
his strength
the weapon used against me
i shook in his presence.

he seemed to be isolated from everything important
he seemed bedless and couldn't think
splintering every time i spoke.

shades of hazel—the color of eyes
well built, smooth skin
executive vice president of a west hollywood bank
both trying to be rational inside a
north hollywood bath & sex breakfast club.
his penis was overly huge and he
parading the steam room
his meat flopping side to side covering a huge sack of
testicles.

i bought a dog when i was fifteen and
i don't know why—i don't know why i thought
about this dog at the present moment
maybe it was his cock
maybe it was the realm of things happening...
he sat down beside me
putting his face between my legs and
perhaps i should have pulled away, but

i let him dominate me then, then
let him dominate me after.

there is a war against self
there is having sex with someone strange
and he asked to dominate my asshole
he's not a bottom

and i say i'm not a top
a match
a perfect connection and within minutes
we were inside a private room and he was
slam fucking me into a mattress
he slam fucked me for four and one half hours
and i was bleeding and bleeding and bleeding
my skin was torn apart, but
i let him continue
i let him have his way
his condom was skin tight, sheer thin, and
i could see his massive meat thru the splitting
rubber.

he told me sex kept him alive and
that i had the best piece of ass he's had
in a long time
he bit my eyebrow and tensed
his sperm shot forth endlessly as
i thought about my gi joe doll, the dharma bums,
and drawings by keith herring.
i wanted to escape the hurt
to stop thinking 'hurt,' so i started
thinking about my favorite movie title
'some like it hot.'

he asked if he could see me again
if we could do this again and i

said sure as long as you understand
'i got the best piece of ass in this century'
he threw the sheet over my body as he got off
his cock was still stiff as if he should continue
but i couldn't do another go
but i couldn't continue at this moment
i was hurting
as my fingers rubbed my asshole and
my asshole was wet from lube/cum/blood/shit.

the fitted sheet was destroyed
the fitted sheet was destroyed
the fitted sheet was destroyed.

(should have meditated—went away)
next evening at his west hollywood penthouse
same routine—same events
not even dinner, not even a drink, not even a smile
just a 'come lets get it going,' then
he slam fucked my body until i was
breathless—until i couldn't move
and his rubbers tore
and his rubbers tore
and my asshole tore
and his sperm covered my body
and i was bleeding and bleeding and bleeding
the wildness and the rawness
made everything pitch black.

later in bed we talked and i opened myself
and i would've cut my throat if he'd asked
and the myrrh incense reminded me of a catholic church
and his prowess was illuminating
and i asked about AIDS testing
and he just looks at me and smiles and smiles and says
'My last test was in 1985 and it was positive'

and it was positive
and it was positive
and it was positive
and it was positive
and echoes and echoes
and echoes and echoes
and echoes and echoes.......
the lights got dimmer and dimmer
the night got denser and denser and
thought about the rubbers tearing
thought about my asshole tearing
thought about the bond of his cum and my blood
and i couldn't believe he was trying to kill me
with his body
with hatred
couldn't believe he'd fucked me knowing he was
dying from an incurable disease
we were sex partners.
a flash of consciousness
and blood was still between my legs
and blood was still between my legs
and the monster with his huge engine lowered over me
and i could only see death
and the monster murmured a sad harmonium of sounds
'i'm going to take as many as i can with me
men and women/boys and girls.'

my stomach began aching—legs twitching
my last test three weeks ago and
i was negative
i was negative
i was negative
i was clean......
i don't want to die
i don't want to die
and now i may die for my sex life.

he handed me a death sentence
a death certificate
a bathrobe 'clean yourself.'

the fitted sheet was destroyed
the fitted sheet was destroyed
the fitted sheet was destroyed.

a part of me fell in love
loved him then, but now he's a monster
he's a vigilante
he's a destroyer
he's a devil atop a silent skyscraper, crackling,
a television airwave vibration—a carrier.

walking out he asks me 'can i see you again before
i retire and move to thailand?'
whatever happens to me will happen to all the others
whatever happens to me will happen to all the others
whatever happens to me will happen to all the others.

an immaculate space of hollowness draped in camouflage
thru my shoes out the door behind me
and i knew another test must be scheduled
and i knew i may become untouchable
and i knew i must tell my boyfriend.

i'm writing this about death
i'm writing this about the chaos of flesh
i'm writing barely able to sit down
i'm writing this because i'm dealing with it...

the damned have no minds
the damned have no minds
the damned have no guilt
ALWAYS PROTECT YOURSELF.

'PENETRATION SHAME TWO: HISTORY'
FROM THE PERFORMANCE WORK HEAT (1993)
KEITH HENNESSY

One of my brother lovers got a phone call, "You might have syphilis. Go get tested. Call your friends." And he did, and then I called another brother in L.A., and we all got tested. This is community. Friends and strangers who penetrate each other; who enter each other; who get off together. At city clinic they treat us when they test us, in case they never see us again. Penicillin to the butt. Ooh. "And we might as well treat you for gonorrhea and chlamydia while you're here." A shot to the shoulder and bright blue pills. "And if you have all these diseases you could have HIV. When was your last test?" "OK. Let's do that too," I comply. But of course, there's no treatment for that. For hours after that we're grumpy; hashing out inconsistent details in our information; wanting more research on precum; evaluating our personal protocol.

ALTITUDE
MICHAEL JOHNSTONE

The elevator takes forever to get to street level. I think of velocity, an elevator does seem slow compared to the speed of life at fast forward. The sky is a pale mist of darkening blue, and strands of fine white hair. A pink cast intrigues the shadowlight of faces at the bus stop. Faces full of life, uncertainty, tired, hollow, wide awake, vacant, aware. Huddled quickly onto this bus. Traveling at a high speed onto the expressway, time again disappears into velocity and a jumble of sensibilities. When was he last able to ride a bus? When was he last able to climb the stairs? When had we last met for dinner? When did he forget what my name was?

A PRINCE OF LOVE IN EVERY WAY
BRIAN BOULDREY

Once, there were two men who were at an earlier time in their lives very much in love with each other, but they weren't any more. But they did live together, and they hatched moneymaking schemes together (which usually failed), and they shared things in the refrigerator together (not just milk, bread, and orange juice, but anything that happened to be there), and they quizzed each other's prospective suitors when they came to the door for a date. This last thing they called "getting rid of the shoe salesmen." Naturally, therefore, they were both single.

They both worked for the theater, behind the scenes: Sal, the shorter Mediterranean one, was a dresser, and Doug, the tall blonde one, did makeup.

One day, Doug found out he had the virus in him, and although Sal never got tested, he assumed the same was true of himself, since he shared so many other things with Doug.

Among the things that Doug lamented because of the virus, one was the fact that he feared he would never know what it was like to be old. He stood one morning in the kitchen doorway, wearing a ratted terry robe, contemplating the sharp knives porcupining out of the dish rack. Sal walked in and Doug asked him what he was trying to do, kill him?, while pointing at the fan of treacherous blades in the silverware crock. "There are enough opportunistic infections to fight without having to avoid flesh wounds," he said. "Do you know what will probably happen to me? I will never get pneumonia or meningitis, I'll be nickeled and dimed to death instead. I'll get pinkeye and croup and acne and amnesia and ingrown toenails, and then one day I'll be stung by a bee and my throat will swell up from an allergic reaction and I'll never actually get diagnosed. An ignoble death!"

Doug was obsessed with ignoble death. In his childhood, his pet terrier, Gretel, fell into a hot tub and drowned. He had tragic memories of finding the dog's silky hair splayed like an anemone on the frothy surface. Doug's favorite poet had been hit by a dune buggy on Fire Island. His mother ate a bad crab burrito.

"What kind of death isn't ignoble?" Sal wanted to know. His eyes hurt and he was weary on this late October morning, and he was waiting for the coffee to start working on his system. During this Halloween season, he used his theatrical costume abilities to bring in a little extra money making complicated dresses for drag queens, and ended up working late into the nights, ruining his eyesight like a Balzacian poor relation laboring over fine handmade lace. He was finishing the hem on a costume dress this morning, and Doug could hear the sound of Sal's fingernails scrape against the fine pink silk.

"Death with your wits about you," Doug said. "The ideal death would be one done in battle over a true love whose name had been besmirched and needed to be cleared."

"I'd settle for death after a good lay," Sal said, pulling a needle up out of the dress, "or a decent single-malt scotch."

Doug sat at the kitchen table with his own cup of coffee and stared at the gown, a strapless number, piled and ribbed like wedding cake frosting in Sal's lap. "Well, I'll tell you one thing, I wouldn't want to die in that dress. That's an ignoble death."

"That's your opinion," Sal said, "I know a half dozen guys who'd *die* to get caught dead in one of my creations."

That's when Doug got The Idea. It was another one of his moneymaking schemes. Sal knew Doug had one of his moneymaking schemes because he had seen Doug get wide-eyed before, but he'd not seen him so excited since the time when he had the idea for the come-towel delivery service scheme (they'd deliver them like diapers to gay men's doors fresh weekly on a subscription basis, the soiled ones picked up in a convenient sanitary blue laundry bag). "What's on your mind?" Sal said warily.

"With your costume ability and my expertise at makeup, we could start a service for ailing men who want to know what it would be like to be senior citizens. We get them up in loose baggy clothes and I make up their faces to look like shriveled prunes, then we give them an itinerary of bars and potluck suppers for the geriatric set. Then they can get an idea about what it's like to be old, even if they never get a chance to live that long."

"You're sick," said Sal. "Besides, who wants to be old? I have enough trouble attracting men the way I am now," Sal was always skeptical, and never stopped hemming.

"Can't you imagine for a minute what a relief it would be not to be vain?" Doug said. "No, I suppose *you* couldn't. But Sal, you wouldn't have to worry about being desirable any more, you could save all that time spent primping in the mirror. People would love you because you were lovable, not because you were hot-looking."

That morning, Doug talked Sal into trying it with him. The two of them took all afternoon finding clothes that were unfashionable. Doug meticulously caked on pale, waxy makeup to simulate huge cartilage deposits, created little inserts for the nostrils of gray hairs that looked like fly-fishing lures to the naked eye, and mixed up lotions that wrinkled the skin when they dried. They found wigs that made them look like they were balding and unkempt, and they practiced hobbling a little—not too much—with a cane.

In the evening, they went to The Galleon for dinner, an oldster's restaurant decorated with twinkling Christmas lights, understood to be stars. They were shown by a kindly and careful young waiter back to the 'Honeymoon Table' where they could enjoy their meal and watch a teenaged singer in a feather boa. They had an after-dinner drink at The Twin Peaks, peering pleasantly into the bustle of weekend Castro traffic, where eyes ogled and leered into other eyes, and Sal and

Doug felt wonderfully invisible—so much that Sal actually enjoyed and tasted his scotch for once. To cap their evening off, they went to J.J.'s and sat near the piano while gay men went through the entire Lerner & Loewe repertoire. There was one song that both Sal and Doug knew well, and they sang along unembarrassed.

"We met at nine," Doug sang.

"We met at eight," Sal disagreed.

"I was on time."

"No. You were late."

"Ah yes," Doug crooned Frenchly, "I remember it well."

They would have sang the whole thing together except that their friend Terry came up and recognized them under their disguises. "Well, if it ain't Maurice and Hermione," he squealed. "What in the hell are you two up to?" He pointed to them and drew the attention of all the adjacent tables.

"Shh," Sal said. He wanted to enjoy his expensive drinks in peace. But Doug wanted to be noticed. He wanted to start his new business. "Terry, you've got to try it. Sal and I are going into the Old-Man-Drag business."

"Old Man Drag?" Terry said. Everybody around them wanted to hear, too.

"Say you don't know when you might get sick," Doug said. "Say you don't know whether you'll ever get to retire at sixty-five. Sal and I will make you up and give you tips so you can spend a night being a senior citizen. For a fee we'll give you an itinerary, an outfit, a face-drop, and a complimentary souvenir cane to remind you of your trip."

"God," Terry whispered. "It sounds tasteless. I've gotta try it. Sal, are you having a good time?"

"Yes," Sal admitted. He really was, too.

Terry watched them and they all sat quietly at the table as the song was finished: "Am I getting old?"

"Oh no! Not you—/ How strong you were,/ How young and gay;/ A prince of love/ In every way!" At first, as part of the play-acting,

Doug and Sal held their canes in one hand and held the other's hand in the free hand. Now they were enjoying holding hands without even pretending. Terry noticed how much they were enjoying things: the music, the alcohol, the knobs on the top of their canes, each other's company. Terry was blonde and stocky, a sort of combination of Doug and Sal. He liked to look as young as possible, and had his hair carefully rumpled under a baseball cap worn backwards on his head, and had t-shirts with naughty sayings printed on them. Tonight, he had one that read, 'Happiness is a Wide Open Beaver' on it, even though Terry had little interest in wide open beavers.

"Say, you guys," Terry said, "when can I get into Old Man Drag?"

"Tomorrow, if you want," Doug said. "But it's going to cost you. Twenty-five dollars a night."

"No problem. I'll be over tomorrow at noon."

That night, Doug and Sal made appointments for four other bystanders in the bar who heard about the Old Man Drag plan. They were impressed with the convincing makeup job. By the next weekend, they had a backup on their calendars and decided to hire Terry as a permanent assistant.

They tried out several names for their company—Gaffers & Geezers, Accelerated Decrepitude, A Mass of Dotage, The Methuselah Society, Artificial Fogey-fication—before they settled on the picturesque but fairly truthful Second Childhood, Inc. Their motto: "Facilitating a May-December Romance!" The business boomed. In just half a year, the client base was over five hundred, and there were many who came in for a second and third makeup session. They sold subscriptions to old age, as to the opera. The clothes had to be returned, but each customer received a special Second Childhood cane as a souvenir of being old.

Doug and Sal liked to wear their makeup on the job, as a testament to their workmanship, although their best advertisements went out into the city, drank drinks at The Mint, played lawn bowling and shuffleboard in Golden Gate Park, took up ballroom dancing, played bingo at the Metropolitan Community Church, and started up a special, highly controversial chapter of the Gay and Gray Club.

By the end of a year, certain bars were known to encourage a clientele that wore Old Man Drag. Also, competition sprang up, but the outfits and makeup provided by Deans & Doyens were markedly shoddy and customers who strayed from Second Childhood soon returned, sheepish. Doug and Sal never let their standards fall.

It was exactly two years later, and the two of them were closing up their swanky shop at 19th Street near Castro. It was a weeknight, so the business was not as crazy. Lately, Second Childhood had been enjoying a popularity among straight women, who wished to look old and less physically attractive in order to escape the catcalls of men on scaffolding and the usual harassment in neighborhood bars. Everybody in the city was discovering the pleasures of escaping the treadmill of desire.

A man had come in the shop just before closing to offer wigs on a wholesale basis, several styles of gray hair in various stages of wispiness. It looked like a good deal and Doug and Sal signed an agreement to receive their first shipment. Sal was behind a desk, in full old man drag, peering over spectacles (which were real, he had finally ruined his eyesight through his sewing) at the terms of the wig document. Doug hobbled around convincingly from the back storage rooms into the section of the shop where the makeup was administered, with barbers' chairs and light-lined mirrors, moving with his own trademark cane, shrunken down into his clothes. Not only his face, but his arms and neck were ash-colored. He said, "Where did I put my glasses?"

Sal said, "They're on your face."

Doug said, "Oh, right." The wig salesman left the store and the little sleighbells jingled as the door shut. Doug sat down contentedly, and Sal went over and put the 'Closed' sign up. Doug sighed. "Who would've thought? Who would've thought we'd make a career out of retirement?"

"Certainly not me," Sal agreed. He took off his bifocals and rubbed his eyes. Doug looked at the mirror and pulled a quarter-size bit of latex off his face.

Sal said, "Don't you want to go out tonight? We'll get a good seat at The Galleon because tonight's a weeknight."

"Naw," Doug said, "I'm pretty beat."

Sal sat down next to Doug. "But don't you know what today is?"

"What? What's today?" He stared at the spots on his hands and thought about Nivea Skin Cream.

"It's our second anniversary. The second year of Second Childhood."

"Wow, I usually remember stuff like that, don't I?" Doug said.

"Yes, you do," Sal agreed. Now he was putting his cane down behind the front desk and he wiped his face perfunctorily with a towel.

Doug said, "Would you mind it so much if we celebrate tomorrow night? I'm kind of tired."

"Suit yourself," Sal said. He came over behind Doug and helped him stand up. Then he picked up the little pillow Doug liked to sit on which made wooden chairs more enjoyable. Then he grabbed Doug's cane and put it back in his hand.

"You're not mad?" Doug asked.

"Nope," Sal said.

Doug's pill box timer beeped in the breast pocket of his shirt; it was time for his pharmaceutical shakedown: retrovir, fluconozol, lysine, One-A-Day For Women (for the extra iron). The shirt sagged with the weight of the pill box. He thought, I ought to buy some smaller shirts, I can afford some new shirts. He said, "Sal, am I getting old?"

"Oh no! Not you," Sal said.

AIDS DEATH #54,911

ROBERT KAPLAN

The last time I saw you, Steven, you were huddled in bed,
blankets piled over your body,
you were shaking and shivering so much
there was nothing that could stop it:
your hands bunching the pillows,
your legs threshing the sheets,
you screaming over and over Lord I want to die
please just let me die.

And I sat cupping your head as if that could do anything
as if there was anything I could do
feed you tea hold your hands give you more blankets
crawl into bed and lie on top of you:
my stomach on your back
my arms around your stomach;
anything to give you warmth, just a little bit of warmth.

It was summer; it was New York; I was back in town
and you were dying. I could sit in waiting rooms
I could help you in and out of cabs and up and down stairs
I could cook for you and wash your dishes and
get you shrimp lo mein I could wrap your neck
with towels soaked in warm water
talk with you about our favorite poets and
that little magazine we used to edit and
how you wanted to be back in Indiana and
everything was over, everything we knew was over.

It was summer, it was New York, it had been a year
since I had left; and you had buried your lover
and you had lesions all over your body
and when I sat in bed with you,
pulled up your shirt to give you a massage
and felt your spine between my fingers
you started crying about the last time anyone had touched you
and how your parents were always yelling,
coming to visit and yelling, blaming you for everything,
and all your friends had deserted you except Michael and Anne;
and Anne lived in Boston and Michael never touched you.

Now Michael calls me and I still do not know why I am healthy
and you are dead. Then Michael tells me how you died:
in a hospital, alone, 32. Yes I can picture that.
I can picture that or the night we sat on your fire escape:
it was summer, a different summer; we were smoking a joint and
you were telling me about a man you had just met
whom you really liked, you really liked him a lot.
Was it safe to kiss, that's what you wanted to know. Steven,
—isn't that just the most awful question: is it safe to kiss?

GARDEN
EDWARD WOLF

With popsicle sticks and white string
I go into the yard
and stake out my garden for the coming spring.

Bearded iris here and cosmos there;
purple alyssum encircling all.

A siren shrieks down Army Street
and I recall
the hiss of oxygen
the sour smell
his yellow hand...

I'll plant some calla lilies,
I'll try some celery
I'll buy some roses
Perhaps some poppies.

The shadow of the fence
creeps slowly by my side
and a breath of wind
as gentle as his last
so smooth, so fine
his face now is there
that place, that peace
I hope it's true...

The sweet smell of onionweed
arises as I kneel
and press my hand

against the earth
his chest
so quiet now...

I take a stick and push–
the ground so easily today
allows;
there's a lot
to measure, to plan.

He would approve.

And he is gone.

THE ONLY ONE IN THE ROOM
WAYNE T. CORBITT

They were strong, weak, loved, despised, beautiful, homely, gracious, rude, sexy, sleazy, smart, stupid, Black, white, brown, and blurred by memorials through veils of tears. These were they, freaky, homoradical misfits, a gentle tribe at home on the wild side. The ism's lose their potency, yet are magnified by the experience of surviving; not just friends and loved ones, but regrets and missed opportunities as well. They were mostly white gay men at first. It was easy to pity from a distance, even though I knew some of them. Then a friend, a Black man, freak like me, got sick and died. Suddenly it was my place, time, and road to tread. As HIV and AIDS spread, being Black, queer, sadomasochistic, and a poet made a difference. The choices I made had a significance to which I'd been blinded. Surviving my circle forced me to seek out new friends, few of whom could understand the isolation I feel or the obsession I have to identify everything. The explanation to those quirks in my character is complicated and (to a point) inexplicable. No one sees the wounds inside.

The reality of being Black in America is that sooner or later you discover we ain't overcome yet. It is glaringly obvious if you move socially in a white world. To protect yourself, it becomes necessary to let small slights pass and assimilate. You're getting along fine, when you glance into the mirrored wall of an upscale bar or restaurant and notice you're the only Black person in the room. As there were fewer friendly ears to share the adventures of last weekend without a shocked silence at the punch line, things changed. I was uncomfortable with the solitude of a crowded room. It became more and more tiresome arguing that HIV is a virus and to blame the infected is unreasonable and unjust.

There was a wild party. We had a good time. It's over. We were all too aware of the low self esteem in which we were generally held, but we are not and never were disposable people. My queer brothers left something behind, people like me.

Being the only one in the room is compounded by HIV in ways so subtle they go unnoticed by the uninitiated. A friend of mine, a white man, gave a dinner party that I cooked for. Two of the guests were Black gay men, one a Black woman of unknown persuasion, and a white gay man. I was acquainted with one of the Black men and knew the others only slightly. All were friendly and polite. During a lull in the conversation, the woman suggested we tell stories. I decided to tell a silly sex story. Years ago I went cruising in the Tenderloin. It was wonderfully sleazy in those days. (There was an obvious prim reception to "wonderfully sleazy.") I'd found some major Black trade straight out of East Oakland looking for a blow job and some drugs. I was cruising for rough trade, someone to fistfuck me (another prim reaction). My major trade gladly shared my drugs; enthusiastically fucked my face, then my ass; but when I suggested he fistfuck me, he replied in absolute horror, "You want me to what?"

I'd told that story over the years. When I told it, my leather friends would double over with laughter. Mark would lose his serious attitude pose. Ron's forced smile would show genuine glee. Martyn would say, "My word, what a slut" through guffaws of laughter.

The dinner guests at my friend's table had no idea the effect of their silence on me; but I longed for the familiar comfort of like-minded companions. In that silence, I was the freak, haunted by the poor skinny sissy boy that I was. In that silence, I was a survivor of a way of life and a culture changed irrevocably. In that silence I was alone with ghosts of the Ambush, Arena, and the Brig, leather bars of my youth. That silence reminded me of my membership in a morbid club which has as its motto, "All my friends are dead." Like Russian

Easter eggs that open to show another to open . . . and on and on, the crowd was shrinking.

One would expect (ten years into the epidemic) some reasonable adjustment would be made to ease the compounded loneliness of being a long term survivor. As my friends were dying in quick succession, whether they were Black or white mattered little. It happened so fast, consideration of loyalties never occurred to me, until all the leather people were dead; then the Black ones, then my lover . . . Along the way I made new friends, but constantly losing history as my old ones passed on. Carrying on is so much work!

But carry on I do, in spite of the guilt and regret that accompanies complicated odysseys, no matter how illogical that guilt and regret may be.

Before the final nightmare, (the wasting and suffering), my companion, David, and I went for a weekend in the country. There was a peace to the quiet on the drive up. David had been diagnosed eleven months, and with the exception of two episodes of PCP, one mild and one (the first) quite serious, he had enjoyed good health. It was 1987, AZT was still torture treatment and the average lifespan after diagnosis was eight-ten months; but we were content and well.

When we reached the cabin, David needed to nap, an event reminding us of the cloud AIDS had become. I made dinner, which he nibbled but never really ate. We smoked some pot and drank some red wine. We kissed and cuddled. He asked to fuck me without a condom. I did not reply. We jacked off, then went to sleep. That night has haunted me ever since. I could not have imagined the depth of the regret that silent rejection echoed. Six years later . . .

I met a lesbian composer and poet of obvious sensitivity. We spent an afternoon together sharing ideas and each other's work. I naively read a poem for her, that included some of my more raunchy verse.

She reacted with self-righteous consternation comparing the pandemic to the holocaust, the pandemic self-inflicted while the holocaust had some nobility. She chose to argue a point in theory that was a passionate reality for me. But she spoke a common belief held by many, that HIV is the fault of the infected.

How dare they assume authority only experience can teach! Gay men sought freedom sexually, and we had no idea that there was a virus somewhere out there waiting to kill us. One more time I defended behavior fostered by ignorance and repression. But what I couldn't say, what I didn't say, what I don't say is I am tired of being the only one in the room; I am weary from the fight. What I don't say is fuck you, you don't know what the fuck you're talking about. You can't know where I've been; that somebody peed on me in the restroom at school, so I learned to hold my water; that straight African-American boys chased and beat me up, so I learned to distrust my image; that the lesson of self-loathing was learned well. Unless you understand where we come from, you can't begin to know what we've come to. Once you understand this lifetime and variations on the theme, you start understanding the behavior condemned by nearly everyone outside that behavior.

I found refuge and camaraderie among the perverse, the decadent and the hedonistic. I was safe with them, running from a nightmare that has no end, only respite. Their numbers dwindled and as they did so, I found myself the only one in the room more and more. Cactus and rose stems have the right idea, touch them and bleed. Someone calls the truth a lie and I sit silent, screaming inside, mourning alone. What I don't do is run shrieking through the street haphazardly condemning to death anyone I deem enemy, oppressor or problem! It's not easy being the only one in the room!

The hardest part is life without my Davey. William David French was to be my lifelong companion. He was a tall, potential porker with red hair, freckles, rabbit teeth and the most beautiful blue eyes I've ever seen. We made a family. With him there was someone on my side, even when we disagreed. I was sure he was there. All through the shock of the first AIDS deaths, we held each other close as life and hope. I was to go first. After all, I was the sickly one, the fragile one, the slut; but it was he. After seven years of struggle, hope, fighting and reunion, we were content.

At two o'clock on the morning of February 2, 1988, I was eating a hamburger when David called me. I walked into his room to see him lifting one pale skinny arm, then the other. "Doing calisthenics," he joked. He could always make me laugh. I fed him melon and morphine, then crawled in beside him and fell fast asleep holding his hand. Around five o'clock his legs, which were propped up on pillows, fell on mine, startling me awake. His breathing changed. He was comatose and had shit on himself so I changed his diaper.

I went to the front of the house to tell Bob and Mark (our friends who had spent the night), what happened and chain-smoked three cigarettes. David could no longer tolerate my smoking in his presence. The three of us then went back to the bedroom after the attendant changed his diaper again. His breathing was labored, holding on as I held his hand and sang 'You Are My Sunshine' in his ear. We used to do the Ray Charles arrangement in two part harmony. Between each chorus I'd say, "You can go now, we love you, it's o.k. to die." He stopped breathing at nine-thirty that horribly pretty morning.

I was euphoric! It was over!

Six months later I began sewing his quilt panel, having only buttons and minor repairs to my repertoire. Suddenly I missed him more than I've missed anyone or thing. Death of the body is permanent. The pain of that knowledge still catches me off guard. That I have survived so many, especially Davey, amazes me. As weak weary fragile frightened and angry as I am sometimes, I am a survivor and I am unsure whether it is a blessing or a curse.

ERASING NAMES
SUZANNE SHERMAN

My address book is filled with so many names of men
who love other men
who love
men that die
so early
still in love

Do I cross out just one name, leave the other
David and Brian, Tede and Chuck
Should I pen in the new address when there is one,
a new home, where maybe the dishes they bought together
will look different
a new home that offers half a chance at letting his spirit voyeur
as a friend, not a haunt,
(feeling like a traitor,
 he touches his lips to a new man's throat)

David and Brian, Tede and Chuck...
How can I cross out Brian? How can I erase Tede?

Boys I cry for you, and I don't know what to do with your names

THE HOLY WAR
NANCY BOUTILIER

What prince of peace is this
Arriving at the gate
With a platoon of pasty followers?
No baggage to claim,
Except his insecurities
And Bible verses.
He has time to spew
Self-righteousness
To the press
And fire off a round
Of born again babble
Before leading his flock
To the funeral.
Already late,
These misguided saints
March to the front
Of the church
Armed with their certainty that
"God Hates Fags."
What is there to protest
In a death
For those who believe
God's will be done?

Inside the church,
Mourners celebrate a life
That ended early,

But not early enough
To keep this fallen soldier
From leaving his mark
On those with ears
To hear.

Unfortunately,
This man
Who lets himself be called
Reverend
Is too busy listening
To his own voice
Declare God's will
To hear the multitude
Lift a psalm to the sky
With eulogies for
And tributes to
The fallen prophet
Whose truth was rooted
In books far too honest
For the man
Who thinks
He knows
God's will.
So, the man
Who lets himself be called
Reverend
Leads his lemmings
Into darkness,
As those he would have
Burn in hell
Walk together
With a faith of their own
Through the shadow
Of the valley of death
Speaking in tongues

That burn with the rage
Of having their hero wronged
By one cemented in the certainty
That he is right.
So blind to his own blindness
Is this man
Proclaiming to know
God's preferences
That he misses the miracle
Before him:
The spirit of the man to be buried
Rises triumphantly
In the sacred songs,
Lifted even higher still
by the choir of fags,
Many of whom
Are so courageous
That God
Perhaps
Not only loves them
But calls them
To His side
One by one.

QUEER QUEER? QUEER!
TIMOTHY BUTTERCUP

It's not about continuing the status quo,
or bragging about who you know
It's not about chest size, dick size, wallet size, or breast size
It's not about money, class, position or status
It's not about GAP, BMW, or living in the ghetto
Forget styles, trends, and pretending to be hetero
It's about brother loving brother; sister loving sister;
brother loving brother
loving sister loving sister
It's not about objectification of bodies
It's about exploration of possibilities, of our heart and soul
It's about drag queens at Stonewall, fairies and leather;
nature and magic, reveling in pleasure
It's not about crystal meth, cover charges, attitude or greed
It's about acceptance and love, truth and healing
It's about fighting AIDS and expressing what you're feeling
It's not about being fabulous at the expense of other people
It's not about red ribbons or those goddamn freedom rings
which buy us all complacency
and make us forget about the important things
It's not about being told where to go, who to fuck, or what to buy
It's about questioning the status quo and always asking why
It's not about 'straight-acting', 'straight-appearing', or self-hatred
It's about breaking the ties that bind us and giving something back
It's not about living a lie and putting on an act
It's about taking what's rightfully ours and never selling out
It's about fucking and kissing, sucking and fisting
Queer means no apologies to anyone, no fear, no assimilation

WHEN STRAIGHT MEN TOUCH
LEWIS DESIMONE

A touchdown pat,
a homerun embrace.
In the euphoria of victory,
the hypnotic endorphin hour,
skin touches skin—
disembodied as alcoholic words,
lost memories of lampshade hats.

In daylight,
in moments of rawer emotion—
Pain, fear,
the things we don't admit-
the skin hurts,
like a sunburn,
too delicate to be touched.
But for safety's sake,
for ego's preservation,
we call the weakness strength
as each settles into his corner.

AUGUST 31, 1986
RICHARD LORANGER

August 31, 1986 was my last day as a bicycle messenger in San Francisco, a life I'd been living for nearly two years. I'd reached a panic stage in my life-change neuroses and quit, having no notion what to do next. I might have seen a flashing sign—DANGER PROCEED WITH CAUTION—in the events of that very night, had I been looking. But how often are we looking when the boulder falls?

I went to a big messenger party at 20th and Capp—a full moon night, luna lluena in the Mission. Those days as ever messenger parties were wild excursions, frenzied things, shrieking ripped jean roadrash affairs, power chords and flying skateboards, dirty hair, chain grease, pounding walls, fights and sex, black leather, psychedelics, utter folly, silly music, loud music, whatever drugs at hand, and beer, beer, beer, busted hydrants, giant tits of cheap beer. I spent hours crammed on the little back porch, smoking section for this monstrous bash, yelling and smoking and drinking and drinking and drinking Budweiser from the can, blood full of moon. Staggered off with Malcolm near 2 a.m., I too drunk to ride my bike, he flying on three hits of acid, to his apartment nearby where we both could crash.

At 20th and Mission ending the 25th hour of the day astride the omniscient Hunt's Donuts, we were approached by two cholos for marijuana. Nope. Dissatisfied with this level of interaction, the inquiring gentleman suggested that Malcolm and I were lovers, and with a distinct air of distaste, inquired if this were the case. We were not, in fact, lovers; though we were, in fact, going to sleep together that night;

and, in further fact, we had several years prior once engaged in sex. So this question proved more complex than actually intended, particularly to our addled minds. Discerning our confusion, the gentleman collared Malcolm (a good 6' 3" to my 5'9½"), and demanded he admit it.

Malcolm, acid bubbling in his veins, started yelling in his face in Spanish.

The gentleman was kind enough to show us his knife, yelling, "Say it in English! Say it in English!"

Joyously, repeatedly, Malcolm confessed our queerness en Espanol, which the man, to his shame, did not understand. Somewhere in there the second gentleman smacked Malcolm in the mouth, bloodying his lip. I backed off a couple feet, sober to the bone, wondering if this would end before I swung my Kryptonite bike lock, a distasteful measure at best. Instinctively I said, "C'mon, Mal, let's go." They were still arguing. I repeated.

Then, strangely, they paused. Malcolm turned and said, so slow and strangely, "I can't, he has me by the shirt."

An odd thing happened—as if he'd pointed out an obvious faux pas, and dignity demanded the situation end, the impassioned gentleman released my friend, and we walked into the rapid night, shaky and unscathed.

BUSSING
ELISSA PERRY

It was shortly before six on a Friday evening the sun had set but it was not quite dark. The bus was crowded but silent. Everyone watched as the 49 crossed the 33's path and stopped to change its load. Shit, I hope I make that bus. We waited anxiously for the 33 to pull across the intersection and open its back door. I guess I could walk. I looked down to survey my outfit and my don't-mess-with-me attitude. I had walked up Mission Street countless times alone in the past looking much dykier than this without even a second thought but this time it just didn't seem right.

Finally, the 33 driver decided to break the Muni law that prevented him from opening the doors when not at a designated stop, and opened the back door. As soon as the green light over the door was illuminated a crowd led by two teenagers, a male and a female, in matching red jackets spewed from the 33 into the 49.

Once again the bus was packed and once again no one spoke. Everyone seemed to be making the mental transition between where they had been and where they were going. The teenagers in red, no longer boy and girl but not quite man and woman, were silent. The women, done with their day jobs and going home to their familial night jobs, were silent. The teenagers, done with basketball, cheerleading, junior achievement and hanging out were going home to eat with their families before going out to raise hell, were silent. The only noise on the bus was change clanking in the fare box and transfers ripping from the stack.

Three more people got on. The door closed and the driver prepared to pull into traffic. The last three passengers found an open space to stand next to me separating my seat from the back door. I felt more comfortable with a more obvious dyke who was also Latina next to me. Her outfit consisted of a white t-shirt interlocking women's symbol earrings, freedom rings, a leather jacket, hand cuffs, Levi's, and Doc Marten's. Besides a backpack she also had two girls about 11 and 12 with her.

Everyone began to relax, especially the two white people living in an 'ethnic' neighborhood so they wouldn't have to explain their trust funds. We were on the inside of a moving vehicle, an illuminated capsule, looking out through shatterproof windows.

We had not even made it a block when our illusion of safety was destroyed.

"Don't stop at this stop, man."

We stopped accelerating.

"I'm telling you if you stop it's gonna be trouble."

We coasted.

"Man, somebody's going to get hurt." We were about to cross 19th Street and the boy/man in the red jacket was yelling directions to the bus driver from the back of the bus.

The shoulders of the passengers began rising towards earlobes as we stared straight ahead hoping the driver wouldn't complete the stop. The bus ceased to move. Everyone nervously looked around. By now the boy/man was half standing and looking out of the windows. "What did I tell you? Don't stop!"

"Pedro, this is where Jose got shot!" His friend started talking, adding to the sense of impending doom. Half listening to her, I watched the two groups of young men approaching the bus from either side.

No one was waiting at the stop and no one made a move to get off. The bus doors stayed closed and we sat. The young men began surrounding us with bottles and hands ready to reach inside jacket pockets.

A police officer, a rather pudgy pasty man, walked into the restaurant across the street.

"This is where me and the boys got jumped with Diana." The young woman continued reciting the recent history of the corner of 19th and Mission. We sat, listened and watched. The police officer ordered his food, and people kept driving by, more people went in and out of stores picking up last minute things.

Pedro was standing in the middle of the bus not knowing what to do with himself. "Man, what the hell are you doing up there, just go!"

The young men were passing signals around the circle with their heads and eyes and hands. They prepared. We sat.

"Come on, man, go." Pedro was pleading with the driver's forehead in the rearview mirror.

"They pulled us off the lines. We ain't going nowhere," the driver said still staring straight ahead.

"Aw... Shit." Pedro went back to his seat and put his head down between his hands.

Two of the guys began trying to pry the back door open from the outside with their fingers and a stick. The lesbian moved a few feet towards the front with her nieces leaving only air between me and the back door directly to my right. The cop picked up his food, took it to the back of the restaurant and sat down to eat.

The driver laid on the horn.

"Why don't you call somebody?" The white guy with the nylon briefcase, wire rim glasses and leather jacket suggested as if the driver couldn't think of that on his own.

"The phone doesn't work when I'm off both lines." He was a medium brown black man in his late twenties who looked like a giant teddy bear. He was the type who did everything he was supposed to do in high school, had a few friends, modestly played a sport, and waited 'til at least senior prom to have sex with his girlfriend. He was a

Mama's boy. He was still trying to work by the rules of his employer rather than the rules of the street. Both were a reality in his mind although we all thought him stupid at the time.

The teddy bear continued blowing the horn. A handful of people poked their heads out of various storefronts to see if there was an accident.

One gangster reached down for another bottle while another began reaching inside his jacket. I hit the floor. Other people had the same reaction. The aisle and the spaces between the seats and became a human carpet—two layers deep in places. Fingers were stepped on, groceries smashed, bags kicked. No one cared.

Bottles and other objects began hitting the sides of the bus. Pedro and the young woman were silent. Everyone else was cussing and yelling, "Stay down."

I could see the whole fucked-up scenario in my mind. Us laying on the floor having paid a dollar for service that gets shittier as it gets more expensive, the pig stuffing his greasy face with greasy food watching us like we were on *Miami Vice*. I saw the mayor cutting after-school programs, libraries, Muni, $25 million in health services, and planting pretty imported palm trees along the new unnecessary street car line, and the governor cutting $1.7 billion from the Department of Public Health in addition to whatever else he can do to please the Republican Party. They were all saying let them kill each other. The Spics, the Niggers, the Chinks, the Queers, the Commies... all of them. Let them die.

Our tax dollars at work.

The bus driver made his big move. He opened the door and bolted down to the pay phone near 20th to call the police.

The back door was opened from the outside. Two gangsters stood blocking anyone from exiting. The oldest-looking one came through the front door and stood with his legs apart, his gun down protecting his manlihood.

Pedro stood. "We gon' see this out, man, cuz I'm sick of your ass, but let these ladies off the bus."

The gunman said nothing. Several members of his crew were standing behind him lining the front stairs of the bus.

"I'ma be here," Pedro said. "Just let these people off."

We began standing with heads down, shoulders hunched, belongings clutched in front of our chests and filing off the front of the bus. We had to go one at a time, single file, to fit in the stairwell with the gangsters.

"Don't look up," the gunman was saying repeatedly. "Don't look up. Don't look at my face."

I was concentrating hard on not looking up and not falling down. I was hyper-aware of everything. Later, people would ask me what I saw. Shoes, jeans, and the floor. A floor I would recognize anywhere. Dent in the middle of the left side of the metal wall to the right of the stairs, crack coming from the bottom right hand corner of the same wall beginning to splinter, old blackened bubble gum on the right side of the second step equidistant from a barely recognizable silence=death sticker on the left side, drop of dried blue paint on the bottom stair.

I was off the bus. I still didn't look up. I kept moving.

A half a block away I raised my head completely. The bus driver had finished at the pay phone and was running past me back to his bus. I could still hear glass breaking. I did not look.

The dyke and the girls were in front of me. "Mama, did you see that gun?"

So, these girls were her daughters.

"Mama, did you see when those bottles hit the window?" They were jumping up and down on either side of her.

"Whatever you do don't tell your father about this or he will definitely take you away this time."

"We won't, Mama. We didn't tell him about the last time either."

We were about two blocks away when we heard the gun shots. I looked but couldn't see anything. My subconscious had planned it that way.

I walked another block and finally heard a siren. One singular siren.

I walked another block before the bus passed me. He was flying down Mission Street not even pretending to think about stopping.

Would anyone file a report? I wondered.

By the time I made it to El Rio, it was dark, the safe sex workshop planning meeting was over, and the oysters were all gone. I dropped my bag on the floor, propped myself up on the bar, and ordered myself a drink.

An Apocalyptic Update on the Coat of Many Colors
Horehound Stillpoint

i was on this bus
going nowhere special
not doing nothing
when a large body suddenly stood before me
wearing the ugliest damn plaid coat man ever made

like looking at a car wreck
i couldn't take my eyes away
purple and red
black, green and yellow
this thick polyester thing filled my world
my god, i thought
my god
somebody designed that
somebody chose those colors
somebody ran up a test patch
somebody approved the pattern
somebody sunk some money into this thing
people worked on this fabric
in some industrial hellhole
people fashioned this material into coats of many colors
people made wisecracks and watched the clock
they grumbled and sighed and talked about their lives
people planned their days around this stuff

this plaid had a history
the pattern was coming alive
polyester touched my heart

my god
my god
the sun, the breeze, the fog drifting in
giggling children
a piece of plaid
sidewalk trees, seagulls in the sky
the smell of hot greasy french fries

i can't wait, came a voice from the rear,
for AIDS to kill all these fags

well shit, i thought
words to match a purple plaid

you know, if god is
e v e r y w h e r e
he has no taste

ON A CITY BUS
JONATHAN BRACKER

Your hand holding that library book
Might in my hand be held, or stroked, or kissed
If we could speak and you your bus-stop missed,
My having found the way by hook, by crook,
To neighbor you who, maddeningly, look
Not across the aisle and never back. My eyes insist
Insistently but you resist.

I only need to ask what is that book.
Instead, I lick dry lips and seethe and swear
This solitude I play has little joy.
I would give up all this fantasy
If I could only think how one so fair
Could not my lips so happily employ
Which have nothing else to say of you and me.

THE WIND COMES UP AT DAWN
TOBY BIELAWSKI

The wind comes up at dawn
Rolling the sun along on her tongue
With a yawn
The wind is a wild-haired woman
The kind who doesn't mind her own business
The kind who wears a long loose dress
And comes in the window with a violent kiss—
The wind is still young.

The wind comes up at dawn
Spraying water from her frantic hands and hair
On the indifferent gulls
The heaving docks
The abandoned embarcadero.

Do Iguanas Have Forked Tongues?
S.F. Jane

I basked in your attention. Our perfect world was round with a
delicate concavity, like a kidney-shaped swimming pool. That's the
shape my hands around your waist traced, round belly up sides to press
my palms into the depression of your spine. Or the mound we'd make
under my quilt, curled close side by side in sleep, belly to back.

Distrustful of the complacency of happiness, we were determined
to challenge each other, deeper and darker, positive that any change in
either of us would be a further delight to the other. Mine started as a
sexy idea, a daydream really. What if I had..... this.

Before I ever met you, I traveled in Mexico. A trip that got long
and strange, complicated. But one very good day I spent studying
ruins, going from structure to structure with no one else around but
the iguanas. They scattered around in charming poses for me. Beady
eyes, slowly blinking multiple eyelids. Great thorny crests around
their faces. They stayed in my mind for various reasons, iguanas and
other lizards.

With you it was safe to let my imagination wander. You encouraged
me beyond reason, beyond shame. I burned with it in the strange
places it took the two of us, my face hot. You grounded me, a kite-
string on my flights of fancy. Lightning could strike me out there.
You'd hold the charge. I wanted to be like a desert creature which
survives the desolate and the harshly beautiful places. I wanted their
spiky spines, and to make others have the same feelings about touching
my skin.

I thought I knew who I wanted to be and how I wanted to be seen,
but they were only your eyes I thought of, my dark eyed lover. Other
people we knew were getting tattoos, piercing their bodies. I was a
little afraid, but with that breathless excited fear which feels like sexual

anticipation to me. I've cultivated fear in arousal, it's always been that way for me.

I was apprehensive about telling you that I wanted you to do it to me, afraid you wouldn't want to. But you were gravely thrilled when I asked you. Of course it had to be you. I considered doing it myself, but I was afraid I'd slip up and then I'd have myself to blame for botching it up. I was sure you would execute it perfectly, and you did. It's a perfect cut.

I healed quickly. You tended my wound dispassionately, like a nurse when I was in the hospital once, discreet around my sick and stinking body. It seemed more graceful to heal alone, and then to surprise and seduce you when it was finished. I sunk into meditative days with the pain of cut flesh healing. I did not speak, saving my first words after the fact for you.

For all you know this may be lies, as in my bitterness and sense of injustice, deception and lies are what I have come to know best. You will no longer have anything to do with me, but the young girls are all after me, ravaging and drama on their minds. They move in briefly, leave as soon as they get jobs.

Why did you scar me and then leave? When I saw you on the street, in front of the dry cleaners near my house, there wasn't a bone in my body that wasn't ringing true with pure desire. You hadn't come to see how my wound was healing but I had nobly attributed that to some wisdom of yours about letting me reform myself alone, so I could come to you when I was ready and lash your reserve with my wildly erotic new thing.

I was too surprised to speak. You didn't look happy to be running into me in front of the dry cleaners. Anyway, my tongue hadn't healed enough for me to speak very well. So I stuck out my tongue, my beautiful forked tongue, which you had said would be so cool, which your hand so expertly sliced for me.

And you said with disgust, "You're sick."

My Perfect Androgyne
Trebor Healey

He hated being cute
wanted to be tough
pierced up and tattooed
leathered and bootblacked
with those big brown doggy eyes

He hated being cute
I assured him his body
was anything but—
that lithe, snake-like chest
and that stingray of a belly,
those athlete's legs
and soothing sisterly hands,
and his tiny male ass—
that handsome, unmistakeably tough
cock
as hard and undiscriminating
as the policemen's billy clubs
that didn't want his HIV status
stopping traffic

I think of all the lives
it's just run over
unmistakeably tough
and I think of all the goddesses we need
to hold us and to forgive us

Oh Mary, Mother of God
I never feel so close to you
than when I'm in his thin androgynous arms
under the gaze
of those doggy eyes

MR. LARRY, HAIRDRESSER EXTRAORDINAIRE OF MR. LARRY'S BEAUTY BOUTIQUE SINCE 1962, ASKS "WHITHER GAY LIB?"

ALVIN ORLOFF

I was doing my friend Earl's hair the other day when we got to discussing 'Gay Lib'. Earl is of the mind that we homos have been pushed around long enough and ought to get really militant about equal rights and all that. I am bored to tears by politics but I can never pass up a chance to play devil's advocate so I decided to tease him a bit. I said to him, trying to sound sincere, "What if, and I'm not saying it's so, mind you, but just 'what if' the only thing that makes people great artists or scientists or whatever is sublimated sexual desire? What if everybody gets laid whenever they want to and nobody has anything to prove to anyone and nobody bothers to create or discover anything anymore?"

So Earl looks at me like I'm stupid, which is a real laugh since I'm a hairdresser with a nice apartment and he's a barker outside a nudie joint who lives in a dump. "Larry," he says to me, "you're ignoring all the great homosexual thinkers and artists who got all the boys they wanted. Why I bet Michaelangelo got David!"

So I said, "Sure, but he was still an outsider; what if it takes being treated badly to really get those creative juices flowing? Take a look at history. Who's done most of the creative and brilliant stuff? Homos, Jews, and kids from the wrong side of the tracks with chips on their shoulders. You just don't see well-off WASPy, heterosexual guys painting the Mona Lisa or discovering the law of relativity. Oh sure, a few normal types manage to discover or make something nice now and then, but it's the members of tiny oppressed minority groups that do all the really great stuff. Suppose you get your way and the whole world turns nicey-nicey and everyone is treated just fine, but then civilization just stops. Then what? Seems to me being alienated is the only thing that really drives us to fulfill our creative potential."

Well, old Earl just shut up, and I can tell you it's the first time in decades I've seen him without some highfalutin' theory ready to explain just everything. I laughed and told him to forget it 'cause I was just funnin' him, but he looked spooked leaving.

The next time I see him is at the In Touch Lounge on Polk Street. He's cruising some wired little boy and I can't help but have a little more fun. "You know," I say, pointing to the Queer Nation button on his leather jacket (which he *thinks* makes him look hip and young), "you activist types have some pretty strange ideas about what it means to be queer."

"What do you mean?" he says, instantly looking worried.

"Well, back when we were all gay (well, us men anyway) we used to all be fascinated with Broadway shows and Hollywood stars, muscular young men, cross dressing, disco music, and *The Wizard of Oz.* Everyone loved Judy Garland. The gay world used to be a melting pot where differences were assimilated, not into straight culture, but into this weird queen culture. Now things are more mixed up, and different cultures exist side by side and compete for dominance. When one type of homo gets some power, all the other homos resent it and scream, "Oh, he or she doesn't represent me!" The Leather Queens don't care about the Lesbian Separatists, who don't care about the Sweater Queens, who don't care about the Punk Dykes, who don't care about the Radical Faeries, et cetera, et cetera. 'Queer Nation' hah! As if there was one single Queer Nation! The homosexual world is splintering faster than the Soviet Union, and I, for one, say Hurrah! Being queer is just something I was born with or picked up somewhere, it's a characteristic. I want to be judged by my character, what I'm personally responsible for."

Earl then excused himself to run after the tweeked-looking chicken but not before he gave me a condescending glance and promised to have a real long talk with me someday and explain the ways of the world.

The next time I saw Earl was at a leather bar and I was ready for the kill. I'd had a couple of bourbons and was bored stiff. I said, "When I was a kid leather queens were sexy, raunchy, perverse, and sexy. Now we have the 'Leather Community' which is very rich, very dull, very prissy, and not very sexy at all. Look around you, the leather is all new and expensive. Nobody's got that grungy outlaw look that made Marlon Brando so hot in *The Wild Ones*. These guys all look as much like yuppies in their leather outfits as they do in the hateful blue suits they wear in the day! Leather men ought to live in ramshackle clubhouses on the outskirts of town. They're supposed to be ravishingly handsome but woefully inarticulate hooligans. They should never ever live in ugly condos with glass top coffee tables, track lighting, and Herb Ritts prints on the wall. These modern leather queens are so solidly middle class and predictable it makes me positively sick! And the young activist leather kids are almost as bad as the fussy upscale old leather queens. They're so tediously self-righteous. They have the gall to claim their S&M or B&D sexuality is 'transgressive'. They fancy they upset the status quo. Utter nonsense! From the emperors of ancient Rome to Reagan's good friend Alfred Bloomingdale, the ruling classes have always enjoyed sexual games of domination and submission. Society as a whole has been obsessed by macho role playing from time immemorial. Their sexuality is just part of life's rich pageant of psychological absurdity, it's neither unusual nor politically important."

Earl stood mutely waiting for me to finish. Strangely exhilarated by my own diatribe I searched for a new target and turned to the rainbow flag on the wall. "Take the Rainbow Flag, please! Would someone mind telling me why homosexuals, the most aesthetically advanced people on Earth, must be saddled with such a stupid flag? It's so New Age, it just reeks of saving the whales and Birkenstock sandals. We should donate the rainbow flag to Sausalito and make another flag using just our colors, pink and lavender. If we must have a rainbow (in honor of Miss Judy 'Over the Rainbow' Garland, I suppose) I think a pink and lavender field with a rainbow on it and a happy little bluebird flying over would be nice. But that's just my opinion."

Earl lamely giggled, sucked in his gut, and made for some hideous troll who was giving him the eye.

A few weeks later Earl was back at my hair salon for a trim and I had at him again. "I see our Homosexual leaders have been pushing for inclusion in such reprehensible institutions as the Boy Scouts of America and the United States armed forces. Now I don't deny that military life can have a sexy side or that there is fun to be had making sculptures out of popsicle sticks in church basements. I do, however, strenuously object to the way these worthy organizations dress. No self-respecting pervert ought to renounce his or her most precious possession, style, by putting on a uniform just to fit in. I'm especially dismayed by khaki green or brown uniforms. Ugh!!! Earthtones are inherently odious because they aesthetically link humans to the soil and our humble animal origins rather than emphasizing our unique consciousness which makes possible the wearing of dayglo... but I digress. Anyway, fighting for the right to be ill-dressed cannon fodder is not my idea of liberation, especially if it involves getting up at 6:00 a.m. Frankly, the right to be excused from military service strikes me as a privilege!"

Earl had some canned argument about our right to serve our country. Imagine, wanting to be a *servant!*

I switched tactics to confuse him. "When we were kids the hoighty-toighty political types called themselves 'homophiles' and we common queers were considered disreputable, salacious sexual psychopaths; pariahs to mundane respectable Americans. Nowadays, perfectly normal men and women call themselves queer just because they happen to be attracted to members of the same sex. They seem to feel that the pejorative 'queer' lends them a certain sort of glamour: the sultry allure of the outcast. I have no objections to queerness but I am disappointed that just anyone is allowed to claim it, even if they are well paid, law-abiding citizens who agitate for the inclusion of homosexuals in the military."

"So?" said Earl, who can be infuriatingly dense at times.

I next saw my buddy Earl at a cafe in the Castro which was briefly hip during the late '70s and has been living off its reputation ever since. The clonelike creatures who inhabit the place refer to it as Cafe Hairdo despite the glaring fact that any cafe on Haight Street sports more fabulous 'dos. Pretentious, that's what it is. I saw Earl and jumped into my by now familiar pattern of harassing him. "You stroll around your charming neighborhood, wiling away the day in what looks to the casual observer like an idyllic existence composed of brunching, disco dancing, and working out at the gym. It seemed like such a good idea: why not band together in one neighborhood for convenient cruising? Yet shortly after this was accomplished some queen discovered the 'gay market' and men were inundated with iconic images of pretty boys, muscle studs, even centaurs with washboard stomachs, all seducing them into spending their lives and money in the relentless pursuit of pleasure. Every conceivable form of retail and entertainment establishment has been reproduced here in this ghetto making the outside world redundant. Now you see the result, you've all become vain, insular, hedonistic ghetto gays!

"And your ghetto isn't much use to anyone who forgot to be male and either attractive or affluent (or who has too much good taste to let his lifestyles be controlled by cynical and unimaginative gay businessmen). Even white male yuppies aren't really happy here. The pursuit of pleasure isn't emotionally satisfying and it's not a good common value on which to form a community. This," I gestured to the white t-shirted, denim clad throng around us, "is an enervated lot, positively addicted to leather and the rainbow flag. It isn't any wonder their herd-like propensities earned them the nickname 'clones' in the '70s. If you gay libbers want to do something really fabulous you should start by turning the ghettos into places where people of taste and refinement, or even women and ethnically interesting types, can enjoy themselves.

"You Ghetto Gays also have the unamusing habit of trying to out-homo one another. You've lost touch with the straight world and believe all that's needed to attain equal rights is to increase your political militancy. This also makes you look butch and cool, and hence more sexually attractive to other ghetto gays. The worst of this is that you've decided that any consideration of how a particular political tactic is received by the press (and hence, unfortunately, the gullible public) is evidence of assimilation. Tactics guaranteed to incite a backlash are used time and again. It isn't that most politicians and police don't deserve to be boiled in oil; but we're a minority, remember? That means they can lick us in a fight.

"Lord knows, being a minority is no vacation. Yet I'm amazed that so many are prepared to dismiss the majority entirely as wasted protoplasm, 'Breeders'. Well, I for one would like to stick up for these benighted creatures. Many, many heterosexuals, even in the suburbs, are fabulously perverted. Believe it or not, many of the best drag queens are straight. Really! Also 'breeding' produces young people. If they stopped we'd soon live in a world of senior citizens, and who would we have to deliver our newspapers or graffiti the busses?" I stopped for a moment to catch my breath.

"Who would we have to fuck?" intoned Earl, who is a notorious chicken hawk, taking advantage of my momentary pause. "So what are you then?" he asked. "A Republican?"

"Good gracious, no!" I shrieked. "They're worse than any rainbow flag carrying, fussy leatherman, ghetto gay, straight hating, military fetishist who ever lived. Of course 'We' are everywhere and come in all religious, ethnic, and political persuasions. But gays in a political party which is against gay lib? Forgive me if I am too old-fashioned to understand how the desire to support snobbishness, conformity, bigotry, hide bound traditionalism, tedious militarism, and toxic waste could be so appealing that gays would want to overlook homophobia so they could indulge it."

"Then what do you suggest we do about being an oppressed minority?" he asked, for the first time in his life (I suspect), actually waiting for an answer rather than merely waiting for an opportunity to inflict another pat opinion on an unsuspecting listener.

"Lead your life with dignity, style, and an uncompromising dedication to the most fabulous thing you can think of," I replied, sipping my latte and smiling at a boy with blue hair and a silly grin.

STARDUST MEMORIES
BAMBI LAKE

I loved being a teenager in the '60s. I went to see The Dave Clark 5 and
Sonny and Cher once. Sonny had on his shaggy coat and Cher was in
velvet hiphugger bellbottoms with a fur-trimmed velvet hooded jacket.
Cher gave this little child right near me a flower, and I think she must
have also sprinkled me with Stardust because now I'm always around
famous people. Years later my friends and I would go to the Fillmore
to see Janis Joplin, Jimi Hendrix, and Jim Morrison. We'd do acid,
and the girls would get under the stage and listen to Janis stomp. We'd
also go to Be-Ins at Golden Gate Park and buy pot on Haight Street,
but in spite of all that counterculture stuff I still loved musicals best.

FROM KITE HILL WE LOOK DOWN AT THE CASTRO

SIMON SHEPPARD

There, far at our feet,
the roofs and alleys of history
sprawling in the fog. "You can see,"
you say to me, "just where we went wrong."
I squint, adjust my specs.
Still can't see. There, beneath that chimney,
had sex in the kitchen in '73. On that corner,
we gathered after Dan White murdered Harvey.

The birds, I guess, were singing then up here,
as insistently, bravely, as stupidly
as they are singing now. There's where Andy's Donuts
used to be, back before the Castro went all-queer.
After dancing all night to Bowie at the bar,
Charles Isis and John Apple would totter into Andy's,
on platform pumps and too many 'ludes,
for a near-dawn dose of sympathy and sugar.
They're both dead, I guess, like almost everybody else. Dead.
"Where the bodies are buried,
grass grows," someone said.

All the news seems to be bad news,
days like these. Give me your hand, please,
as we two look down as solemnly as stars.
How many down there now,
with their piercings and Doc Martèns,
even remember Andy's Donuts?
So I guess that it's all ours,
old buddy of those days,
the odd-tasting burden of memory,
covered in a melting, sticky sugar glaze.

LET'S KICK FATHER TIME IN THE ASS
MARCI BLACKMAN

i wanna stop time with you
i wanna stop time with you
move within it
surrounded by its stillness
our bodies
twisting and sliding in its deafness
black and white deafness
be still
be still my love my heart
stops beating in time with you

i wanna be still with you
while others scurry about
lost around us
lost
lost in time with you
your hands all over my body
your hands on my back
my ass
your lips on my neck
my breast hardening at the thought of you

i wanna be two with you
for one is cliché
and i never want to be cliché with you
i wanna be two with you
two hearts
two hands slipping in and out of
two bodies
two fluids mixing together
thirsting
unquenched for each other

i wanna stop time with you
move within it
while others scurry about
lost around us
lost in a desert with you
black and white granules of sand
sifting through my hair
my crotch with you
in a desert with you i wanna take peyote
and see the blue monkey

oh blue monkey
indian god of uninhibitions
see the love in our eyes
and lay your blessings upon us
black and white blue monkey dance
dance within us
fill our heads with laughter
make our bodies writhe and scream
in your punishment of ecstasy
craze us blue monkey send us over the edge

i wanna stop time with you
move within it
while others scurry about
lost around us
lost
i wanna kick father time in the ass
then laugh in his face with you
i wanna be two
'cause one is cliché
and i never want to be cliché with you

i wanna stop time with you

Francisco X. Alarcón

NOCHES FRIAS

COLD NIGHTS

sonríes
sonrío:
innecesaria
la calefacción

you smile
I smile:
no need
for a heater

DIALECTICA
DEL AMOR

DIALECTICS
OF LOVE

para el mundo
no somos nada
pero aquí juntos
   tú y yo
somos el mundo

to the world
we are nothing
     but here together
     you and I
     are the world

Contributors' Notes

FRANCISCO X. ALARCON has published nine books of poetry, teaches at the University of California at Davis, and has won numerous awards, including Danforth and Fulbright Fellowships.

CHRISTINE BEATTY is a writer and musician whose first book, *Misery Loves Company*, is a collection of short stories and poetry about her experience as a transsexual lesbian junkie prostitute. She is currently putting together a rock band, *Glamazon*, with her guitar-playing lover, Rynata.

TOBY BIELAWSKI is a Bay Area native and is currently a graduate student in English at Mills College.

MARCI BLACKMAN performs her work frequently throughout the Bay Area. Her most recent book is *Stuck On The Downbeat*.

LUCY JANE BLEDSOE has stories in *Brother and Sisters: Lesbians and Gay Men Write About Each Other*, *Sportsdykes*, *Growing Up Gay*, and *Women on Women 2*.

BRIAN BOULDREY is the author of *The Genius of Desire*, co-editor of the bent literary zine *Whispering Campaign*, and has just edited a collection of essays by gay men grappling with religion, entitled *Wrestling with the Angel*, due from Putnam in 1994.

NANCY BOUTILIER is a high school English teacher and basketball coach whose book of poetry and fiction, *According To Her Contours*, was nominated for a Lambda Literary Award.

JONATHAN BRACKER has had poems in *The James White Review, Mouth of the Dragon, Bay Windows, Gay Sunshine Journal, Gay Literature,* and *The New Yorker;* in three small-press chapbooks; and in the anthologies, *A True Likeness* and *Son of the Male Muse.*

SUSIE BRIGHT has written and edited lots of books.

TIMOTHY BUTTERCUP is a radical faerie faggot poet human being living in the Bay Area.

WAYNE T. CORBITT is an African American performance artist and writer.

DAWN OF AQUARIUS, a.k.a. Priestess of Pop, Queen of the Nile-ists, Goddess of the Go-Go Boys, Hair-o-ine of the New Age, Super Star to the Hairdressers, is rumored among other things to be the long lost love child of Goldie Hawn and Andy Warhol and reincarnated Olympian deity, moved to San Francisco in 1981 from San Diego with dreams of becoming a pop singer, is still working towards that dream, founded *Blondzine* and Blond Nation (a group aimed at ending discrimination against hair color or appearance) authored *Just When You Thought It Was Safe to be a Republican* and *Beyond the Valley of the Idols,* has been performing and writing since the late 1970s and now resides in the Blond Bombshelter and Pagan Pop Wildlife Sanctuary.

LEWIS DESIMONE, a native Bostonian, received an M.A. in creative writing from the University of California, Davis. His work has previously appeared in *Christopher Street,* and he is currently working on a novel that takes place in San Francisco.

JUDITH FAUCONNIER is a native of France. She currently lives and studies in San Francisco.

ANGELA GARCIA is happy with her decision to leave New Mexico for San Francisco, where she writes and publishes and also grows more queer everyday.

DAVID HARRISON is a San Francisco-based playwright/performer. His most recent work, *FTM*, is a solo performance piece exploring the classic issues of death, transformation, and enlightenment-with a twist. It's based on his own transsexual journey from female to male, as well as his personal duel with breast cancer.

TREBOR HEALEY's book, *The Queer Love of Comrades*, is currently in its third printing.

KEITH HENNESSY is a Canadian-born, queer San Franciscan working the fields of radical public sexuality, anarchist empowerment, and ritual performance.

TIFFANY M. HIGGINS volunteers for *Lyric*, a queer youth peer program, and is a bisexual Lesbian Avenger whose recent work has appeared in *The Kenyon Review* and *Prosodia*, the literary journal of New College of California.

CHRISTIAN HUYGEN is the author of the play *Waiting for Godette* and the novella *Radar Angels*. He is currently at work on *Blood*, a novel about incest and vampires, as well as a bunch of short stories about lycanthropy, feral children, ventriloquism, airports, bathrooms and petty theft.

MICHAEL JOHNSTONE was born in Edinburgh, Scotland, came out in platform shoes in Wichita, Kansas before the death of disco, moved to San Francisco at the dawn of New Wave, co-edits the zine *Rant and Rave.*

ROBERT KAPLAN is a New York Jew in exile, yearning to go back and not quite ready to.

BAMBI LAKE is a San Francisco native, one of the beautiful, oversexed, neurotic, highstrung victims of the '70s and '80s.

DONNA M. LANE is a native of San Francisco, a native lesbian, and incurably adorable.

SPARROW 13 LAUGHINGWAND is a radical faery and a warrior witch queen, born 1959 in central West Virginia. Sparrow's books are *Bums Eat Shit and Other Poems, $7 Shoes,* and *The Queen of Shade.*

ALI LIEBEGOTT's most recent collection of love poetry, *I Never Promised You an Opium Den,* is now available.

RICHARD LORANGER, author of *The Orange Book,* has been published and has read around the country for fifteen years, and won't shut up until all minds are clear and free of fear.

AL LUJAN was born queer in East Los Angeles and is currently doing hospice care in San Francisco.

MABEL MANEY was born in Appleton, Wisconsin in 1958. She is the author of the Nancy Clue Mysteries *The Case of the Not-So-Nice-Nurse,* and the forthcoming *The Case of the Good-For-Nothing Girlfriend .*

TEDE MATTHEWS was a collective member/owner of Modern Times bookstore in San Francisco, as well as a writer and artist, activist and organizer. Tede died of lymphoma on July 19, 1993, but his work continues.

MAGGY MERRICK believes comic writing to be more healing than group therapy, though she prefers therapy to most dental work.

JANELL MOON has won three national poetry prizes and writes and lives in San Francisco where she has a private practice as a hypnotherapist. She is co-founder of Sunday's Child, a San Francisco lesbian art salon. She has published a chapbook, *Woman With a Cleaver*.

ALVIN ORLOFF grew up in TeeVeeland and currently resides in San Francisco where he writes for his zine, *TANTRUM*, DJs at Klubstitute (a notorious queer niteclub), and dabbles in low-budget high-camp theater.

ELISSA PERRY recently had a story in the *Girlfriend Number One* anthology. She lives in San Francisco.

STEPHANIE ROSENBAUM is a freelance arts journalist, cultural critic, and spoken word performer who has been living in San Francisco for the past four years.

S.F. JANE lives and writes in San Francisco when she isn't living somewhere else.

CHRISTY SHEPARD is a poet trapped in a social service worker's body, a Midwestern spirit stuck in the Bay Area, for whom writing is a way out.

SIMON SHEPPARD lives and writes in Berkeley.

SUZANNE SHERMAN's first book, *Lesbian and Gay Marriage,* was published in 1992. Her work has appeared in *Bay Windows* and *Common Lives/Lesbian Lives.* She was a contributing playwright in Theater Rhinoceros's 1993 production, *Jumping the Broom.*

IAN SIGNER was born and raised in the San Francisco Bay Area, but didn't officially come out until his senior year at U.C. Berkeley, when a letter he wrote in response to a column was chosen to be nationally published. Since his graduation in Spring '92, he's worked as a naturalist and writer in California, Mexico and Central America.

INDIGO CHIH-LIEN SOM makes artists' books and writes. She is a garlic-chopping S.F. Bay Area bi-dyke Chinese American fire horse/cancer. She's got poems in *Piece of My Heart: A Lesbian of Colour Anthology*, and the title poem in the anthology of Asian/Pacific American lesbians and bisexual women, *The Very Inside.*

HOREHOUND STILLPOINT is the long lost love child of Winnie the Pooh, Barbarella, and Waiting for Godot, dressed in sorrowful '90s rock'n'roll poetry drag.

MICHELLE TEA is a happy Aquarius with a big ego nd three little books: *Oppress Me Before I Kill Again, Tripping On Labia,* and *Heartbreak Cigarettes.*

MERLE TOFER participates in European poetry music festivals, publishes in Japan, France and India, is a Pushcart Award nominee, and studies occult philosophy.

TRAC VU was born in Sai Gon in 1968, and came to the United States at the age of fourteen. He earned a B.A. in English in 1991 from U.C. Berkeley, where he studied writing under June Jordan and Peter Dale Scott.

ROBIN WHITE was born English, is a writer and a freelance radio reporter, currently working on a radio documentary about survivors of the AIDS epidemic.

EDWARD WOLF lives in San Francisco and is currently working on a book of poetry about the AIDS epidemic.

The editors wish to thank
Elaine O'Rourke, Jude Fauconnier, Phyllis Burke,
Eli Coppola, Lisa Taplin, Chuck Barragan, Scott Idleman,
and Jennifer Joseph.

manic d press publications

The Rise and Fall of Third Leg. *Jon Longhi* $9.95

Specimen Tank. *Buzz Callaway* $10.95

The Verdict Is In. *edited by Kathi Georges & Jennifer Joseph* $9.95

Elegy for the Old Stud. *David West* $7.00

The Back of a Spoon. *Jack Hirschman* $7.00

Mobius Stripper. *Bana Witt* $8.00

Baroque Outhouse / The Decapitated Head of a Dog. *Randolph Nae* $7.00

Graveyard Golf and other stories. *Vampyre Mike Kassel* $7.00

Bricks and Anchors. *Jon Longhi* $8.00

The Devil Won't Let Me In. *Alice Olds-Ellingson* $7.95

Greatest Hits. *edited by Jennifer Joseph* $7.00

Lizards Again. *David Jewell* $7.00

The Future Isn't What It Used To Be. *Jennifer Joseph* $7.00

Acts of Submission. *Joie Cook* $4.00

12 Bowls of Glass. *Bucky Sinister* $3.00

Zucchini and other stories. *Jon Longhi* $3.00

Standing In Line. *Jerry D. Miley* $3.00

Drugs. *Jennifer Joseph* $3.00

Bums Eat Shit and other poems. *Sparrow 13* $3.00

So Much for Passion. *Wendy-o Matik* $3.00

Into The Outer World. *David Jewell* $3.00

Asphalt Rivers. *Bucky Sinister* $3.00

Solitary Traveler. *Michele C* $3.00

Night Is Colder Than Autumn. *Jerry D. Miley* $3.00

Seven Dollar Shoes. *Sparrow 13 Laughing Wand* $3.00

Intertwine. *Jennifer Joseph* $3.00

Feminine Resistance. *Carol Cavileer* $3.00

She Knew Better. *Wendy-o Matik* $3.00

Now Hear This. *Lisa Radon* $3.00

Bodies of Work. *Nancy Depper* $3.00

Poets Guide to SF. *Jennifer Joseph* $3.00

manic d press
box 410804
san francisco ca 94141 usa